CALLING CARD

The beautiful woman's face was swollen and discolored. Blood from her cheek and nose ran down her throat onto her blouse.

From under his jacket Zable removed a revolver fitted with a silencer. Crago took a step away. Zable aimed the revolver close to the woman's heart. Then he fired.

She fell twisting against an end table and slumped dead onto the floor.

"Hand me the rope," Zable ordered.

Crago looked down at the body. "She's already dead," he said. "What're you gonna do with the rope?"

"I'm gonna hang her."

Zable reached down and tore off her blouse. He proceeded to remove her clothes until he had stripped her naked.

Crago shook his head. "I don't think she knew."

"She didn't."

"Then," Crago shrugged, "what good did this do?"

"Mulligan and she were close. Very close. This way maybe we don't have to go looking for him." Zable stared at his partner with cold, cobra eyes. "Now maybe he'll come looking for us."

BLOCKBUSTER FICTION FROM PINNACLE BOOKS!

THE FINAL VOYAGE OF THE S.S.N. SKATE (17-157, $3.95)
by Stephen Cassell
The "leper" of the U.S. Pacific Fleet, SSN 578 nuclear attack sub SKATE, has one final mission to perform—an impossible act of piracy that will pit the underwater deathtrap and its inexperienced crew against the combined might of the Soviet Navy's finest!

QUEENS GATE RECKONING (17-164, $3.95)
by Lewis Purdue
Only a wounded CIA operative and a defecting Soviet ballerina stand in the way of a vast consortium of treason that speeds toward the hour of mankind's ultimate reckoning! From the bestselling author of THE LINZ TESTAMENT.

FAREWELL TO RUSSIA (17-165, $4.50)
by Richard Hugo
A KGB agent must race against time to infiltrate the confines of U.S. nuclear technology after a terrifying accident threatens to unleash unmitigated devastation!

THE NICODEMUS CODE (17-133, $3.95)
by Graham N. Smith and Donna Smith
A two-thousand-year-old parchment has been unearthed, unleashing a terrifying conspiracy unlike any the world has previously known, one that threatens the life of the Pope himself, and the ultimate destruction of Christianity!

Available wherever paperbacks are sold, or order direct from the Publisher. Send cover price plus 50¢ per copy for mailing and handling to Pinnacle Books, Dept.17-273, 475 Park Avenue South, New York, N.Y. 10016. Residents of New York, New Jersey and Pennsylvania must include sales tax. DO NOT SEND CASH.

MULLIGAN

ANDREW J. FENADY

**PINNACLE BOOKS
WINDSOR PUBLISHING CORP.**

PINNACLE BOOKS

are published by

Windsor Publishing Corp.
475 Park Avenue South
New York, NY 10016

Copyright © 1989 by Andrew J. Fenady

All rights reserved. No part of this book may be reproduced in any form or by any means without the prior written consent of the Publisher, excepting brief quotes used in reviews.

First printing: October, 1989

Printed in the United States of America

for Cousin Pete in La Quinta
here's "what could happen if..."

and for Toledo's North Enders
especially THE FAHTASHs

and for Mary Frances
who didn't take Dean Schwab's advice

Chapter 1

The early afternoon sun burned onto the corner sign, making the shimmering letters difficult to read.

JASON LEWIS FORD
YUMA'S FINEST CARS
NEW—USED

The side door of the display room was opened and held open by Jason Lewis, a well-built man in his early forties. Lewis' glossy blue eyes were shielded by a pair of Porsche Design sunglasses. The eyes were just watery enough to warn of too much accumulated vodka. But Lewis had not had a drink that morning. His sandy hair was styled with a studied unstudiedness. His smile featured perfectly capped teeth. He wore a lightweight blue sport coat, pale custom shirt open at the throat, and dark blue trousers. Despite the fact that shoeless he stood six feet tall, Jason Lewis wore shoes with inch and a half lifts.

Claire walked through the door that Lewis held open.

His smile broadened as he slipped his hand onto the fluent curve of her hip. While his eyes were a trifle watery, hers had the touch of frost. Claire was at the peak of her beauty. A redhead, thirty-seven, white velvet complexion, she wore a clinging white summer dress, red silk scarf, and red shoes, leading up to long, well tapered legs.

There were dozens of automobiles on the lot. Jason Lewis escorted her toward an immaculate blue Lincoln Town Car.

"What do you feel like, Claire?" He clipped his words like an Americanized Cary Grant.

"Cool, crisp salad, white wine and then...."

"Yesss...?" He stopped walking and placed his hands at each of her elbows.

Her fingertip touched the small gold medal attached to the slim gold chain he wore at his throat, then lightly traveled down the two unbuttoned buttonholes of his shirt. "What time do you have to be back?"

"I'm the boss, remember?" Lewis pointed to the sign, still playing it like Cary Grant—or George Hamilton.

"Then ...," Claire purred seductively, "we'll go home."

Gently, Lewis guided her closer to him. "Let's skip the salad and white wine and go directly to ... Boardwalk."

"Why, Jason," she playfully pulled away, "someone would think we weren't married."

"Can't help it if you drive me wild."

"Like last night?"

"And this morning. And right now."

"Let's get out of the sun before I freckle."

Lewis opened the passenger door of the Lincoln and Claire slipped in smoothly, showing a lot of leg.

He closed the door, walked to the driver's side, and got in. He placed a hand on her left knee and worked his palm upward on her inner thigh as he leaned close to kiss her.

Just as their lips touched, a baseball bat held by a pair of strong, knotted hands smashed the windshield.

Lewis and Claire broke apart. They could see the figure of a man standing outside, but his face was not discernible due to the damaged pane.

The man stood casually near the hood of the Lincoln, holding the baseball bat as it if were a walking stick.

Lewis flew out of the car roaring. "Are you out of your goddamn mind!"

Clair opened her door and looked at the man.

"Mulligan!"

Mulligan was not smiling. Not frowning. As usual, his face was as close to expressionless as an expressive face can be. Not an overly big man. But big enough. Calm, creased, confident, with steel gray, knife-blade eyes that were twin danger signals. And, as usual, he spoke softly.

"Lovely town Yuma. Nice place to visit, but ..."

"What're you doing here?" Lewis demanded.

"You take a man's wife, that's nothing." Mulligan pointed to Claire. "She takes my money, that's larceny."

"I had a right to that money." Claire edged back a bit.

"Half of it," Mulligan replied. "The law says fifty-fifty. There was twenty grand in that account. You owe me ten."

"Have your lawyer call us." Jason Lewis adjusted his Porsche Design sunglasses with his right thumb and middle finger.

"Naw." Mulligan shook his head ever so slightly. "Let's talk it over."

He swung the baseball bat down on the Lincoln's hood, creating a massive dent.

"Jesus Christ!" Jason Lewis exclaimed.

A buffalo of a man wearing a jumpsuit and carrying a clipboard came out of the repair section. He looked and walked like someone who welcomed trouble. Jason Lewis looked glad to see him.

"What's the problem, Mr. Lewis?" Buffalo inquired.

"No trouble," Mulligan responded. "Just talking things over."

Buffalo seemed to become disproportionately larger as he came closer. He came to a halt about ten feet away from Mulligan and stood with his feet planted wide apart. Not a very smart stance, Mulligan automatically noted.

Buffalo looked at the damaged Lincoln, then at Jason Lewis, then at Mulligan. "Who is this guy?"

"I'm the Louisville Slugger," said Mulligan.

"Yeah? You drop that bat buddy and we'll talk things over."

"Like this?" Mulligan let go of the bat.

Buffalo smiled, dropped the clipboard, and strode toward Mulligan, his hands already turned into fists.

Mulligan kicked the bat, which had landed at his feet. "Catch."

The bat flew up toward Buffalo who instinctively reached out with both hands. Mulligan bobbed low, then shot a right cross to the cleft of Buffalo's chin. Buffalo dropped like a hanged man through a trap door.

Mulligan reached down near the benumbed man and

retrieved his bat. He looked at the herd of expensive automobiles as if he were selecting his next target.

"Jason, pay the son of a bitch!" Claire flared. "He's crazy! You don't know him like I do!"

"That's a fact," Mulligan nodded.

"I haven't got that kind of c-cash," Lewis stammered. "It's all tied up in inventory."

"I'm a reasonable man." Mulligan pointed toward a new shiny red Bronco. Loaded. "I'll take that Bronco."

"That machine sells for sixteen thousand!" Jason Lewis exclaimed.

"I'll throw in my wagon," Mulligan motioned with his bat toward a discolored, waffle-bodied Chevy station wagon. The only things about the vehicle that seemed to be in respectable condition were the Utah license plates.

"Get rid of him, Jason." Claire squeezed Lewis's arm. "Just get rid of him! I'll make it up to you."

"Hey! Hey!" Mulligan winked at Jason.

On the cement, Buffalo was beginning to regain consciousness, but he had the good sense to remain immobile and out of harm's way.

"Jason, *please*," Claire implored.

"All right. *All Right!*"

Mulligan dropped the baseball bat near the inert figure and almost smiled.

"Nothing left but the paperwork."

Chapter 2

Two hours later the Utah license plates were attached to the shiny red Bronco heading north with Mulligan behind the wheel. He had a Montecruz cigar stuck in his mouth and was humming "Home on the Range" through the swirl of smoke he exhaled.

Mulligan pressed a button and the driver's window slid up. Then he pressed a button on the dash and caught Nat King Cole in the middle of "To the Ends of the Earth."

"Ah, Claire," Mulligan sighed. "All is forgiven."

But it wasn't. And not forgotten. You don't forget almost seven years of storm and strife. During that time they had been apart almost as often as they had been together. He deceiving and killing for his country—and the money. And Claire becoming more impatient and passionate between each of his assignments.

He had been a hero at war and afterward, risking his life in places she couldn't remember or pronounce—Skopje, Eregli, Nicosia, Skikda, Tabriz, Benghazi, Tequcigalpa—places everywhere, just as in the song the King was singing, "To the Ends of the Earth."

At home he didn't want to be heroic, except occasionally in bed. But for Claire, occasionally was not enough. She was insatiable. Teasing, taunting, tormenting, and always wanting more. Excitement, money, and sex. Claire didn't care if Mulligan loved her—just so he made love to her and bought her the stuff that sweet dreams are made of.

Even now he could hear her voice, the words she spoke to Jason, just as she had spoken them to him hundreds of times. "I'll make it up to you."

Whenever she wanted something—the more outrageous and unreasonable, the better she kept her promise—"I'll make it up to you." Mulligan could picture Claire right now making it up to Jason Lewis. He'd get his ten grand worth and then some.

But Jason Lewis was just another link in Claire's chain. She was too much for him, too much for any one man. There had been other links before Mulligan, and Mulligan himself had lasted almost seven years, but that was because he was away so much of the time, making the world a better place for his country—and his country a better place for the world.

And then it would be back to Claire and those frosty eyes. But that was all of her that was frosty. The rest was hot and hollow.

The mellifluous, unmistakable voice of Ol' Nat King Cole was singing, " 'A thousand goodbyes won't convince me you're gone.' " Well, Claire was gone, and Mulligan hadn't even said goodbye. He'd just mounted the Bronco and blew.

Mulligan hit another button on the dash and waited a reasonable time. Nothing.

With the cigar still clenched in his teeth, Mulligan muttered. "That sonofabitch—the air conditioning doesn't work!"

Chapter 3

Mulligan was still moving north on 95, through Needles, past Boulder City, and toward the city with few clocks and no locks on the casino doors. The city with wheels of fortune and, more often, misfortune. The city where you could get odds on anything from birth to death, to whatever happens in between. Suckers' Paradise. He glanced at a sign on the side of the highway.

> WELCOME TO LAS VEGAS
> VISIT
> The Meadows Hotel
> "Where everybody smiles"

On the radio a local talent calling himself Smiling Jack was making a pitch while flying a helicopter over the patchwork of pools, tennis courts, golf courses, hotels, motels, casinos, pawn shops, and wedding chapels that bloomed out of the concrete garden of the desert.

"Look up everybody—this is Smiling Jack Jordan rid-ing high in The Meadows Hotel helicopter. The Meadows Hotel 'where everybody smiles.' A beautiful day in Las Vegas. A balmy ninety degrees. Clear and clean. The traffic is light. The track is fast, and most of you lucky pilgrims are heading for The Meadows Hotel—'where everybody smiles.' "

But Mulligan wasn't heading for The Meadows Hotel. He'd check in at a motel that would cost half as much and be twice as quiet.

The white limousine pulled up at the porte-cochere of The Meadows Hotel. The chauffeur, a mediterranean man in uniform, got out and moved toward a rear passenger door.

The chauffeur's hand reached for the door handle, but a black hand beat him to it and eased the door open.

The mediterranean man moved as if to shove the black man aside, but reconsidered when the black man, handsome and square built, flashed a Las Vegas lieutenant's shield.

From out of the cool, dark interior of the limousine stepped an expensively tailored man. Mr. Albert was in his mid forties, with the requisite expensive jewelry and slight continental accent. Mr. Albert was followed out of the interior by a flawless blonde. Too flawless. She looked as if she had been taken apart and reassembled by an expert. Everything was seamless and symmetrical.

"Mr. Albert." The lieutenant spoke just above a whisper. "Let me speak to you in private."

"Why?"

"To save us some embarrassment."

"I am not easily embarrassed."

"But I am," the lieutenant replied. "And so is my partner over there." The lieutenant discreetly nodded toward detective Joe Rodriguez who stood near an automobile, as detectives will.

The lieutenant led Mr. Albert a few steps, stopped near a pillar of the porte-cochere, and spoke quietly.

"Mr. Albert, you are not welcome in Las Vegas."

"I have reservations at this hotel."

"Not anymore. Nor at any other Las Vegas hotel."

In spite of the lieutenant's low-key voice, the blonde and the chauffeur could hear the conversation, particularly Mr. Albert's words.

"What's your name?" Mr. Albert demanded.

"Lieutenant Bernard Browne—Browne with an *e*."

"Do you know how much money I spent here during my last visit?"

"We know *everything* about your last visit."

"What do you mean?"

"I mean you have two options. Get in your car and leave Las Vegas. Or get in my car in handcuffs and answer a complaint I have on file."

"How much money do you make?"

"Millions. Ever been handcuffed, Mr. Albert? Very undignified."

"You can't scare me."

"There's a little boy's father who's looking to kill you."

"Nigger son of a bitch!"

"You've got ten seconds to decide."

"Black bastard!" Mr. Albert hissed.

Lieutenant Bernard Browne produced a pair of handcuffs.

"Five seconds."

Mr. Albert turned quickly on his heels, moved toward the car and snapped at the chauffeur. "The airport!"

He got into the rear seat and slammed the door shut, leaving the blonde standing outside while the chauffeur hurried toward the driver's side.

The blonde rapped her knuckles against the window. Mr. Albert pushed a button and the window slid down.

"What about me?" she said.

"What about you?"

"My luggage." The blonde pointed to the trunk.

Mr. Albert reached out and handed her a fat wad of hundred-dollar bills, then instructed the chauffeur. *"Yulla!"*

The limousine's engine energized and the car's tires spun, propelling the machine out of the driveway toward the strip.

The blonde stood looking at the money, then at Browne. "Is it all right if I stay?"

"Enjoy your visit." Browne smiled.

The blonde put the money into her purse. "Damn foreigners."

She turned and walked toward the entrance, swaying in perfect symmetry.

The voice came from behind Browne's back.

"Want to try running me out of town, black bastard Browne—with an *e?*"

Lieutenant Bernard Browne absorbed the words for a moment.

Detective Joe Rodriguez, who had heard the challenge, was heading toward Mulligan to put the arm on him as Browne turned, a wide grin already on his face.

"Mulligan!"

Browne waved to Rodriguez just in time.

"It's okay, Joe."

Browne put both arms around Mulligan and hugged him close. "You crazy sonofabitch!"

"Careful, *Ber*nard." Mulligan always pronounced Browne's first name with emphasis on the first syllable. "Your rod is bruising me."

In slow deliberate motion, Mulligan playfully arced a right-hand shot to Browne's chin as Browne smiled and moved his head with the punch.

Chapter 4

Lieutenant Browne went off duty early that afternoon to mix a few drinks and memories with Mulligan. Some of the memories were spoken; others remained unsaid, played out in the minds of both men like a montage in the movies.

It all began that time in Toledo, Ohio, when Bernard's father, who had a small print shop on Canton Avenue in a black neighborhood, had sent his fifteen-year-old son to make a delivery of meal tickets and menus to the Presto Lunch on St. Clair Street near the Cherry Street Bridge. On the way back Bernard was jumped by three older kids from the north end's Slaughterhouse Gang. They smashed Bernard's bicycle and were trying to do the same to his head, when Mulligan waded in.

Mulligan also was from the north end, but he didn't belong to any gangs. He belonged to himself. It was Mulligan and Browne back to back with bloody knuckles, and when last seen three guys from the Slaughterhouse Gang were running north toward the Buckeye Dump, where they'd lick their wounds and concoct a story about being ambushed by six polacks on Stickney Avenue.

That was the beginning of Mulligan and Browne. They did a lot of things together and played high school football against each other, Mulligan for Woodward, Browne for Waite. After quarterback Mulligan broke backfield Browne's tackle and scored the game's only touchdown, Mulligan jumped off the Cherry Street Bridge into the muddy Maumee River to celebrate. Browne jumped in too, for no apparent good reason, except for the fact that he could swim better than Mulligan. The rescue squad came after both of them, but they didn't need to be rescued. They just needed a bath.

They went to different colleges, but to the same war.

Mulligan was an officer, but no gentleman. Browne was the toughest top sergeant in that or any other company. They took turns saving each other's life until Browne got a battlefield commission and was given his own platoon.

On their last mission together they went in without orders to get Mulligan's brother-in-law, an Air Force captain who had been shot down and caught by Charlie just behind the lines. They found Tom Robbins with both his eyes burned out, his genitals cut off, about ten minutes away from bleeding to death, begging to die.

Mulligan put his pistol to Annie's husband's head and squeezed the trigger. Neither Mulligan nor Browne ever spoke about it since.

Fifty thousand dead men later, not counting the enemy,

when the politicians had had enough of undeclared war, Mulligan went into Intelligence and Browne became a cop. Sometimes they'd hunt and fish together near Salt Lake City, where Mulligan's sister Annie had moved and where Mulligan had met and won his wife Claire. Browne never married, unless you could consider a badge a wedding certificate.

And now they were finishing dinner in a restaurant at The Meadows Hotel. A waiter stood ready to refill the coffee cups.

"Will there be anything else, gentlemen?"

"Just a little more coffee, Max." Browne nodded.

Mulligan shook his head, 'no more.' Max poured for Browne, then drifted toward another table.

"So you traded Claire in for a Bronco," Browne said.

"No, she traded me in. Wanted some excitement."

"Mulligan," Browne smiled, "you've been accused of a lot of things. Dull isn't one of them."

"It is lately. I quit, remember. And I didn't quit rich. That Bronco constitutes most of my estate."

"At least it's paid for," Browne observed.

"Yeah. In case I die in Las Vegas, see that my sister gets it, will you?"

"Why should you die in Las Vegas—how is Annie?"

"Got to die some place, how's any young widow?"

Max appeared with a check, but before he could set it on the table, a man's well manicured hand reached in and took it.

"I'll take that, Max." The hand was attached to Johnny Rice, who was also well barbered and tailored and smelled good. Next to him stood Louis Lepitino, who did his best to look, dress, and smell like Johnny Rice.

"Better not, Mr. Rice." Brown smiled. "Might look like a bribe."

"Your friend here a policeman?" Rice inquired.

"No."

"Then I'm picking up *his* check."

"Mulligan," Browne said, "this is Johnny Rice. He owns The Meadows."

"Not quite. I've got partners. This is Louis Lepitino." Lepitino nodded an acknowledgment.

"He a partner?" Mulligan asked.

"Not quite," Rice answered, then looked to Browne. "Lieutenant, I want to thank you for the way you handled that Albert situation. Very discreet."

"It's my job."

"You're good at it. Most people aren't. You staying at The Meadows, Mr. Mulligan?"

"Why? You want to pick up that check too?"

"Any friend of Lieutenant Browne's gets comped."

"Not this friend. Got a swell motel down the street."

"Maybe next time," Rice smiled, too nice a smile. "Thanks again, Lieutenant."

Mulligan looked at Lepitino who still stood silent.

"Nice talking to you, Louis."

Both Rice and Lepitino walked away as if they had something urgent and confidential in mind.

"Mulligan," Browne laughed, "you haven't changed a whit. Still go out of your way to win friends and influence people."

"I'm not running for mayor. Hey, how's Louise?"

"She's out of town."

"I didn't ask you *where* she is, I asked how she is."

"Louise is fine."

23

"Does she still want you to marry her? Or has she come to her senses?"

"Well you see, Uncle Mulligan, it's like this..."

"Yeah, I see. It's none of my beeswax. Aren't you through with that coffee?"

Chapter 5

Mulligan and Browne threaded their way through the herd of gamesters in The Meadows casino, none of whom had a smile on his or her face.

Mulligan had been around a lot of gambling places, as a kid in Toledo at Jimmy Hayes's 631 Club on St. Clair Street, behind the Boys Club in the alley, at George's Cigar Store, in army barracks, then in Saigon before it become Ho Chi Minh City, in London, Paris, and Monte Carlo.

The amateurs, the losers, were always in a hurry, in a frenzy. They couldn't wait to roll, or drop a bet or make a play. The faster they bet, the more they lost. The pros took their time, played at their pace. They were in no hurry. Sometimes they won, sometimes they lost; but there was only one real winner. The house.

Mulligan never gambled. Except with his life. Even then he played the odds. He did everything he could to reduce the risk. He found that the best way to reduce the risk was to depend on yourself. The fewer people you had to count on, the better your chances.

As he got older and looked back at the chances he had taken, he knew he was lucky to be alive. And someday his luck had to run out. He woke up one morning trembling. That's when he made the call to Keyes in Washington. Mulligan spoke just one sentence—"I'm out of it"—and hung up.

He looked around at the people in The Meadows casino, at the money and chips dropped onto tables and into slots, thousands, tens of thousands of dollars being devoured by dealers, croupiers, and machines.

People of assorted ages, sizes, and colors were crowding and shoving as the would-be winners elbowed each other for table and slot space.

"Bernard," Mulligan said, "looks to me like you traded in one crap shoot for another."

"This is nothing, the real action starts later."

A fat lady whirled from an infernal machine, mad. "Shit!"

She bounced into Browne, who was caught off balance and glanced against a thin old lady at another slot.

"Watch it, buster," the old lady growled at Browne.

" 'Scuse, me, ma'am," replied the contrite cop.

Outside, the warm summer wind sighed against the miles of variegated neon streams and bulbs that lit up the streets and city. Night lights, blues in the night lights that spelled out Welcome Pardner. Lights that spelled out sweet love to honeymooners in bed, and mounting desperation to losers at crap tables.

Mulligan and Browne came out of a door and walked slowly toward the parking lot. It was an easy and comfortable walk for two friends who had often walked and sometimes crawled the paths of danger and death, dirty, sometimes bloody, their lives dependent on each other so often that their reflexes seemed like part of the same nervous system.

"Mulligan, I wish you'd change your mind."

"Nope."

"Get you a good job with any of the hotels. I know all the fellows in security."

"Gee, would I get to wear a uniform again?"

"Be serious."

"I've had serious, remember?"

"What are you going to do, hunt? Fish?"

"It takes money to buy bullets and bait."

"There's plenty of money around here."

"Bernard, it's just not my kind of town."

Browne stopped and put his hand on Mulligan's arm for just a beat.

"You're all wrong. Ninety-eight percent of the people here are just like people somewhere else. Matter of fact ninety-eight percent *are* from somewhere else."

"Bernard, get this. I'm *going* somewhere else."

As he spoke, Mulligan, in a slow, deliberate motion, playfully arced a right-hand punch to Browne's chin. Browne grinned and moved his head with the punch.

A shot rang out. The bullet barely grazed Browne's head and crashed through a car window. Dazed, Browne dropped to the cement. So did Mulligan as he looked up and saw the muzzle blast of a rifle firing again from the half-finished skeletal structure of a building across the lot.

The second bullet punctured a tire of a parked car. Mulligan rolled Browne behind the shield of an auto and out of the line of fire. He cupped both hands on Browne's face.

"Bernard?"

"I'm ... okay."

Mulligan reached inside the detective's coat and pulled Browne's gun out of its holster.

"Mulligan ..."

"Bernard, you still need a baby-sitter."

Mulligan bolted from car to car making his way toward the unfinished structure, where the sniper had fired from an upper level.

Chapter 6

Mulligan made it to the dark side of the unfinished building, flattened against a crane, and looked up.

A figure scrambled down a set of stairs. The mediterranean chauffeur was out of uniform. He wore a dark blue suit and carried a rifle. He stopped at the exposed edge of the construction and looked below, toward Mulligan, at the crane.

The chauffeur aimed and fired the Armalite M-18 fitted with a night scope, and missed. He cursed and kicked over a heavy barrel of iron bolts which showered down hard, some even causing sparks when they landed. Mulligan rolled under the cover of a truck. The metal bolts rained into and around the truck; then the heavy barrel plummeted through the windshield.

Mulligan crawled out and spotted a cable suspended near a power box. He wrapped the cable around his arm and hit the switch. Another shot rang out, but missed the moving target. The cable and Mulligan ascended considerably faster than it would take to climb the stairs.

The chauffeur fired again and so did Mulligan, from midair. He swung from the cable and leaped onto the structure.

The chauffeur found cover and aimed the Armalite, waiting for Mulligan to appear. Mulligan stalked through the steel anatomy of the building and stopped just as the chauffeur fired again, this time barely missing Mulligan's head. Mulligan fired back out of the dark. But suddenly it *wasn't* dark.

Mulligan was bathed in the brilliance of a police car spotlight from below.

The chauffeur shot at the exposed target, Mulligan ducked, fired back, and, as the sniper recoiled, shot down directly into the police spotlight, shattering it to shards.

The chauffeur started moving toward a stairwell. Mulligan stepped out and squeezed the trigger.

Click!

The metallic clap was just loud enough for the chauffeur to hear. He turned, aimed, and fired. But Mulligan in a seemingly suicidal leap was diving off the structure toward the ground.

Mulligan fell several stories through the thick night air, air not nearly thick enough to slow his descent—or prevent his death. His body plunged faster and faster and would have smashed onto the stone-hard ground except for the safety netting.

He had instinctively made note of that in case of an emergency. His empty gun and the chauffeur's bullets qualified as just such an emergency.

The chauffeur waited for the sound of Mulligan's body striking the ground, but it never came. When he had waited long enough, he cursed again and started toward a stairway.

He stopped abruptly when he heard another sound—an elevator was being activated below. It was a small, temporary cagelike chamber used by inspectors in the course of the construction. The chauffeur moved to a power box. He allowed the elevator to nearly reach the floor where he stood, then he hit the switch, stopping its ascent.

The chauffeur placed the Armalite on a girder, picked up a pair of heavy shears and cut the elevator cable.

The cage snapped free, plunged downward, and crashed.

The chauffeur smiled the smile of victorious satisfaction and reached to retrieve his rifle. He barely had a hand on it when he heard a scraping noise. He grabbed the rifle and turned toward the sound.

Mulligan hurled the six-foot iron rebar like a lance. The shaft tore into and through the chauffeur's midsection. Almost two feet of the missile protruded from the chauffeur's back. He staggered in shock. There was a final blast from the Armalite that shot off toward the stars; then the weapon fell from the chauffeur's hands as he pitched backward over the edge of the structure. His fall was also broken. Before he hit the ground, his still impaled body was gaffed by the gleaming iron teeth of the enormous crane.

Mulligan walked to the edge and looked down at the slack body hooked into the jaw of the crane, and illuminated by the desert moon. Then he looked at his hand. It was steady. He rubbed the cheek of his face with his knuckles. For a warm summer night his face was singularly cool.

It occurred to Mulligan that he felt better than he had in a long, long time.

The police had set up a cordon to keep gawkers to a minimum, but some personnel from the hotel, including Rice and Lepitino, had gathered near Lieutenant Bernard Browne who leaned on a hood of an automobile. Joe Rodriguez was next to the lieutenant as Mulligan appeared bearing arms. Mulligan handed Rodriguez the Armalite.

"Here's a message from Mr. Albert. Sometimes you have to kill the messenger."

"The chauffeur?" Browne asked.

"Himself." Mulligan nodded and handed Browne his gun. "You ever hear of a full clip?"

"Target practice." Browne smiled.

"So was I," said Mulligan.

"Mr. Mulligan," Rice took a step forward, "are you all right?"

"Sure. This night air is very salubrious."

"Well, Mulligan," Browne smiled, "looks like you're going to have to stick around town for a while." He holstered his piece and turned to Rodriguez. "Get out an APB on Albert."

"I'll lay you eight to five," said Mulligan, "that Albert's not only out of town but out of the country. Maybe Monaco, Paris, or the Casbah."

"Do it anyhow," Browne instructed Rodriguez.

"When you catch him," Mulligan said, "call me. I'll leave a forwarding address. Bernard, you look good with your hair parted on both sides."

"We'll get you to a doctor," Rodriguez assured Browne.

"Want to come along?" Browne asked Mulligan.

"Going to bed. I can't stand the sight of blood." Mulligan walked away.

"Lieutenant," Rice looked at Mulligan then at Browne, "let me ask you something..."

"Yeah, I know." Browne smiled. "Who is that masked man?"

Chapter 7

Mulligan stopped at a liquor store, then pulled the Bronco into a HANDICAPPED parking space at the second-rate motel where he was staying. He walked toward his room carrying a sack with a bottle of Glenfiddich in it.

Twenty minutes later he had showered and was sitting naked on a Naugahyde chair, smoking a Montecruz cigar, by a table with the open bottle of Glenfiddich on it. His body was still lean and firm, and the wetness accentuated the scattered collection of scars he'd accumulated over the years throughout the world. At least there was no new wound tonight.

Mulligan sipped his scotch and spoke into the telephone.

"It's a little late but I figured you'd be watching Johnny Carson, as usual..."

Mulligan's sister Annie was in her bed in Salt Lake City sipping a mug of tea, watching Johnny Carson. Even in a nightgown, it was evident that she had a well-formed figure to go with her attractive, blue-eyed face rimmed by short, blond natural ringlets. A picture of a younger, happier version of her being embraced by a uniformed army officer was nearby on the bed stand. She pressed the remote control button, lowering the volume of Johnny Carson's voice.

"And as usual," Annie smiled, "alone. Just me and my tea."

"Annie, get married again."

"Swell. Maybe the Mulligans can do a double wedding. Tell you what, you find me a guy and I'll find you a girl."

"Should be easy. Hell, you've got the greatest legs in the world, and I've got—"

"Never mind! Speaking of legs, did you find Claire?"

"Yup."

"And . . . ?"

"And what?"

"Did you get the ten?"

"No I settled for a six . . . cylinders, but it's a four by four."

"Is that army talk or Company talk or what?"

"It's 'or what.' You'll see when I get there."

"When's that?"

"When I get there," they both repeated simultaneously.

Annie laughed, then asked, "How's brother Bernard?"

"Right now brother Bernard's having some repair work done on his bumper."

"His automobile? At this time of night?"

"No, on his head. One of the occupational hazards of being a detective."

"Were you there when it happened?"

"Yup."

"Anything happen to you?"

"Nope, I ran all the way home."

"I'll bet. Did I ever tell you you're a crazy sonofabitch?"

"Watch the way you talk about our mother—"

"... But I love you. By the way ..."

"Why does there always have to be a 'by the way'?"

"Are *you* alone?" she asked suggestively.

"No." Mulligan looked at the bottle. "I've got good company."

Annie laughed again. "I know you never say goodbye, so at least say good night."

"Good night Annie."

In The Meadows casino, the "real action," as Browne had put it, was now going full bore. Whatever distraction the gunshots outside the hotel had caused a couple of hours ago might as well have occurred a couple of years ago. No one was really affected except Browne, temporarily; the chauffeur, permanently; and Mulligan. The effect, if any, on Mulligan was inconclusive.

If New York was the big apple, then Las Vegas was the big pizza with all the toppings. Bite into it and forget your troubles, get happy, get loaded, get laid, get rich—then get lost.

Right now there were hundreds of people in the room concentrating on the "get rich" topping. Among the few people not gambling were Harry Kemp and Squeaky Monahan. They were making their way toward a door marked PRIVATE.

Harry looked like a third-string high-school athlete two

decades removed, and was. What you couldn't tell by looking at Kemp and those crocodile eyes was that he could calculate the room's take almost to the dollar. He would have been handsomer without the mustache, but he thought it made him look like Tom Selleck.

Squeaky Monahan, as usual, was a half pace behind Harry and a full head shorter. Squeaky walked on the balls of his feet, had a deviated septum and layers of scar tissue around both eyes, mementos of his bantam-weight days when he was thrown up against too many young, hungry Mexicans and blacks who moved faster and hit harder.

The two men opened and walked through the door marked PRIVATE, entered an anteroom where a secretary worked during the day, and crossed to a more ornate door that was unmarked but locked.

The ornate door led to Johnny Rice's ornate office. It had been decorated by a decorator with good and expensive taste, just as Johnny Rice's wardrobe had been tailored by a tailor with good and expensive taste.

Rice was at his desk on the phone. Also in the room were Louis Lepitino and Louis' younger brother Artie, who opened the ornate door in response to Harry's knock.

"Artie, *buona sera.*" Harry greeted.

"Wie geht's." Artie responded. "Whatayasay, Squeak?"

"Save your money." True to his name Squeaky sounded as if he had a rusty hinge in his throat.

Johnny Rice nodded and glanced at the open briefcase on his desk. The briefcase was filled with neat stacks of hundred-dollar bills. Rice spoke into the phone.

"Yeah, Mr. Keelo, I'm looking at it right now."

Phil Keelo was in bed covered by a silk sheet from his

bulging waist down to his bandy, hairy legs. He looked toward the bathroom and the naked figure of a woman stepping out of the shower and toweling dry.

"So am I," Keelo grinned.

"Sure I get it." Rice laughed his obligatory laugh.

"No *I* get it. But when I'm through maybe I'll ship her down to you." Her glistening silhouette was faintly illuminated by the glowing red, heat lamp from above. Her back was to Keelo, her moist hair coiling gently on soft, wide shoulders. She narrowed to an angular stem of a waist and rounded to smooth, polished hips that forked to long elegantly curved legs. She moved with the grace of a dancer but had more body profile than dancers do. Her breasts were firm but much too large for a ballerina. Keelo devoured the sight of her for a moment, then spoke into the phone again.

"How's everything at The Meadows?"

"Fine," Rice said, then added, "you might read about a little excitement, but we'll see that the papers play it down from this end."

"What kind of excitement?" Keelo looked again at the naked figure now framed in the doorway and facing him. In her right hand she held a towel that touched the floor. Slowly she lifted the towel and tucked the ends across the upland of her breasts.

"Somebody tried to kill a cop," Rice was saying.

"It happens." Keelo grunted.

"This time it didn't," Rice went on. "Harry and Squeaky are on their way tomorrow morning. Should be there the usual time. If there's any hitch you'll get a call."

"No hitches," Keelo decreed. "No calls. Just business as usual."

"Sure, Mr. Keelo. There'll be—"

Keelo hung up and watched as she walked through the shadows and stood close to him at the side of the bed. Very close. She unfastened the towel and let it drop to the carpet.

A small butterfly was tattooed on her upper thigh.

Keelo's face creased into a grin as he peeled back the silk sheet.

"All right, butterfly. Let's see you flutter."

Johnny Rice's thumbs snapped the briefcase shut. He never could recall having the last word with Keelo. He rarely could recall finishing a last sentence without Keelo cutting him off or hanging up. What Johnny Rice could recall was when his name was Reizglowiz during the freezing winters and soggy summers of Pittsburgh, where his steelworker father died too young after years of trying to cough his lungs clean from the corrupt air of the mill. He could recall his mother afterward, always in an alcoholic haze, making less and less sense, drinking more and more rye. But that didn't last too long and neither did she.

That's when Jan Reizglowiz moved to Chicago, became Johnny Rice, and got a job in a cigar store on Clark Street. At first he swept and mopped the floor, cleaned the toilet, washed the windows, and ran errands. Then he sold cigars and cigarettes. Then he moved to the back room where Phil Keelo, who owned this and a string of other places, took notice of the young hustler. The back room was Johnny Rice's crash course in the better things in life. There the suckers could bet on anything in or out of season—baseball, football, basketball, fights, horses, dogs, and elections.

Johnny Rice served his master well, and himself. Clothes, cars, manicures, massages, and women. But there was always the nightmare that one day he'd wake up and be Jan Reizglowiz again. So Johnny Rice never complained, criticized, had the last word, or finished the last sentence. So what? He was still Johnny Rice.

"I don't know how Keelo keeps track of all those dames." That was the extent of Rice's stricture.

"He doesn't," Harry Kemp gibed. "After a week or a month he can't even remember their names."

"Yeah, well he remembers money," Rice said. "Squeaky, did you get the car checked out?"

"Sure, it's brand new. That baby could go to the moon if the road was paved."

"Yeah, well it only has to go to Chicago," Rice replied.

"And back," Harry Kemp smiled.

"I don't care about back." Rice carried the briefcase to a large wall safe. "Just so it gets there."

"Squeaky and I have made the trip so many times we could do it in our sleep," Harry assured him.

"Yeah, well sleep after you get there." Rice worked the combination, missed the last number, and started again.

"What'sa matter, Johnny?" Artie inquired. "Anything wrong?"

"Shut up, Artie," his brother Louis snapped. "What could be wrong?"

"Just asking." Artie shrugged.

Rice opened the safe on the second try, inserted the heavy briefcase, and turned to the others.

"That's it. See you in the morning."

"Hey, Artie," Squeaky said, "you feel like a pizza?"

"Why not?" Artie shrugged again and opened the door. Harry Kemp and Squeaky walked past him, and Artie closed the door from outside.

Louis Lepitino moved toward Rice at the safe. "Anything you want me to do, Johnny? *Is* there anything wrong?"

"No. It's just been one of those days, what with Albert and that guy trying to kill Browne—and there's always the squeeze from Keelo till the delivery gets to Chicago."

"It'll get there, Johnny. It always does." Lepitino smiled.

"Yeah."

"Say, Johnny, how do you think Artie's doing?"

"What's he doing? Opening and closing doors. He want a raise already?"

"No, no. Just making sure."

"He's doing okay."

"We all got to start somewhere."

"It's not where we start." Rice closed the door of the safe. "It's where we end up that counts."

"Right," Louis Lepitino agreed.

The air conditioner in Mulligan's motel room was hitting on about half its cylinders that night. Mulligan had gotten up once and turned it to "high." The result was that the room temperature dropped one degree to about seventy-nine. Still, Mulligan couldn't complain. He had slept or tried to sleep under much worse conditions. In jungles and deserts, sometimes under fire and sometimes in the dead of the night with the dead of the night, their smell getting stronger, but still Mulligan would not move, could not move for fear of giving himself away.

During some of those nights, to pass the sleepless time he would try to remember the names of all the girls with whom he had ever had sex, and the occasions. From the first girl in Toledo until Claire. He knew a lot of guys who did that. They even bragged about the fact that there were so many encounters they couldn't even count them, much less recall names and places.

Then one night in Beirut as he lay thinking about the girls and in which order they came, a night before he was to undertake a deadly mission for Keyes who was sleeping peacefully in Washington, D.C., a terrible thing happened to Mulligan. Instead of remembering and reliving the girls he had had, be began remembering and reliving the men he had killed.

And there weren't only men. He had killed women too, and children—where villages had to be wiped out in order to be "saved."

Of course he couldn't recall names or even faces, but too indelibly inscribed on the tables of his memory were the circumstances that translated into a body count.

Mulligan hadn't killed anyone or anything in just over a year. He'd even quit hunting. Oh, he still would go with Bernard and the other guys to the cabin near Bear River during the season, but he'd never kill anything. He'd fish a little but that was about it. The others realized the change in Mulligan but never said anything.

When Claire found out about the change, she said plenty. She said Mulligan had lost his guts, that was why he quit Keyes and consequently quit bringing home all that money for her to spend. She also accused him of losing his manhood, his potency. After a while Mulligan quit trying to prove to Claire that he hadn't.

But tonight he had killed. Without qualm or compunction. As easily and instinctively as ever. Maybe it was because the chauffeur had tried to kill Mulligan's friend. But another terrible thought pushed its way into Mulligan's mind.

Maybe he was born to kill.

Chapter 8

Early the next morning Browne called Mulligan. Browne was going in to work a little late. Did Mulligan want to have breakfast? He did. Did Mulligan want Browne to pick him up? He didn't. They would meet at the Denny's where they'd had breakfast during Mulligan's last visit. Half an hour.

Twenty minutes later Mulligan was driving the Bronco and listening to Smiling Jack broadcasting from the controls of The Meadows helicopter.

"Another perfect day in every way in Las Vegas. This is Smiling Jack Jordan in The Meadows helicopter wishing you all a good morning—or if you're just going to bed, a 'good night.' "

Mulligan looked up and spotted the chopper. At least it was friendly. Smiling Jack kept smiling and talking.

"Did you know folks, that 'Las Vegas' in Spanish means 'The Meadows'—and in any language The Meadows means fun and games. Yes, The Meadows, where everybody smiles. This is Smiling Jack Jordan turning you back to station KLAV."

Mulligan turned into the parking lot at Denny's.

At a private rear entrance of The Meadows a new Buick sedan was parked with the trunk open. From a nearby door out came Harry and Squeaky, each carrying a medium-size suitcase; followed by Johnny Rice, carrying the briefcase from the night before; then Louis Lepitino carrying nothing.

Harry and Squeaky tossed their suitcases into the trunk. Squeaky closed the lid and headed for the driver's side, Harry for the passenger's side.

As Harry got in, Rice handed him the briefcase. "Don't break any laws getting there."

"Who *us?*" Harry arched an eyebrow.

"You know where the speed traps are," Rice went on. "Squeaky, you got a fuzz buster in that thing?"

"Sure Johnny."

Rice closed the door. "Call me tonight and tomorrow night, till you get there."

"I always do, Mother." Harry smiled.

"Never mind the shit," said Rice. "You're outta here."

Squeaky started the Buick and drove off. Lepitino took a step closer to Rice, looked at the departing vehicle, and smiled. "One more time."

"Yeah," Rice nodded.

"Say, Johnny, you realize how much money we've shipped outta here the last three years?"

"What's the difference?" Rice replied. "It don't belong to us."

"True. Well, see you later Johnny. I got to check on a couple items."

Rice nodded and walked toward the private rear entrance.

Louis Lepitino watched him for a moment, then went off in another direction.

At Denny's, Mulligan and Browne sat at a table near a window. Browne's head was bandaged. Mulligan's breakfast consisted of three cups of black coffee, a slice of unbuttered rye toast spread with marmalade, and three strips of bacon.

Browne's breakfast included three cups of coffee with cream and sugar, a large orange juice, three scrambled eggs, ham, home fried potatoes and onions, three slices of heavily buttered wheat bread, stewed prunes, and a side order of sausage links. He was eyeing the leftover slice of Mulligan's rye toast and the untouched third strip of bacon.

"Go ahead and take it," Mulligan said.

"Thanks." Browne did.

"You going to skip lunch today?"

"I don't plan to. Why?"

"Just wondering."

"I got to feed my ulcer." Browne smiled.

"Is that what that bulge under your belt is?"

"Irish humor." Browne slipped the strip of bacon into his mouth.

"Any word on Albert?" Mulligan asked.

"Not yet."

"Not ever."

"Well, at least he won't ever come back here."

"Bernard, you have that effect on people."

Mulligan's Bronco was parked just outside on the lot. A big pickup pulled in and parked close to, *very* close to, the Bronco. The big pickup was driven by a big woman.

"Jesus, Bernard, look at that!"

"What?" Browne set down his coffee cup.

"A dozen empty spaces and that broad pulls up next to me."

"So?"

"So watch!"

The big woman opened her door and its sharp edge greeted the side of the Bronco. The result was evident even from this distance.

"Damn!" Mulligan exclaimed. "I knew it!"

"Listen, Mulligan, I've seen you drive. You don't exactly mother these babies."

"That's different."

"*Sure*. When you shovin'?"

"Pretty quick."

"Let me know where you put your flaps down."

"You can always find me through Annie."

"Yeah, unless you tell her otherwise." Browne grinned.

"Sometime a man's got to be alone ..."

"Yeah ... 'and he's got to do what he thinks is right' ... any more John Wayneisms?"

The waitress appeared. Mulligan reached for the check, but Browne beat him to it. "I'll take it, that'll make us even for saving my skin ...," Browne smiled, "... again."

The recorded voice from the loudspeaker droned through the morning air.

"As you probably know, Hoover Dam is the highest

dam in the western hemisphere, rising seven hundred twenty-six and four tenths feet above bedrock. It is an arch gravity type dam, six hundred sixty feet thick at the base, forty-five feet wide at the top. The dam contains three and one quarter million cubic yards of concrete. Its weight is six million, six hundred thousand tons.

"There is enough concrete in the dam to pave a two-lane highway from San Francisco to New York City, and contrary to any rumors you may have heard, no workmen lie buried within this mass of concrete..."

It was still too early for most of the tourists, but three men stood on the lip of Hoover Dam atop the vast concrete cup that restrained tens of billions of gallons of the water of Lake Mead.

Louis Lepitino, his brother Artie, and Ted Sahadi weren't paying any attention to the spectacular view or the voice from the loudspeaker.

Ted Sahadi was twenty-seven, a year older than Artie, dark complexioned, with shiny black hair and dressed so that the piece he carried didn't show. Maybe he was a distant cousin of the Lepitinos and maybe he wasn't, but the Lepitinos called him "cousin" anyhow.

"Ted," Louis asked for the third time that morning, "are you sure nobody in town saw you?"

"Nobody," Ted answered for the third time and added, "I'm still in San Francisco. Didn't even take a leak in Las Vegas—right, Artie?"

"I picked him up at McCarran and we came straight here, just like you said."

"Make sure you do *everything* just like I say."

"Shit, Louis, don't start that stuff again. Ted and me aren't a couple of kids anymore."

"We'll find out pretty damn soon."

"Come on, Louis," Ted said, "you know I been doing good lately."

"Good isn't good enough, this has got to be perfect." Louis' right forefinger jabbed Ted's shoulder twice. "Now Artie's got the route with all the stops. He knows where to hit 'em. And they got to stay hit—capisce?"

"Don't worry." Ted patted the gun side of his jacket.

"Listen, cousin, I like to worry. When I'm through worrying I'm dead."

"Like Harry and Squeaky." Artie grinned.

"Just remember, this is a once-in-a-lifetime deal, but any mistakes and we're all dead. Get going."

The Buick was ninety miles out of Las Vegas heading northeast. Squeaky drove and Harry sat on the passenger side, his legs crooked over the briefcase that leaned against the bottom of the front seat, just like on all the other trips to Chicago. But this wasn't just like all the other trips.

All his life Harry Kemp had been a second stringer, a second rater. Good enough to make the team, but not good enough to start, hardly good enough to leave the bench unless the game was already won or lost. A good enough actor to get parts in the high-school plays, but never good enough to get a lead. Handsome enough to make it with the cheerleaders, but not with the Homecoming Queen.

And since then, a second or third banana, finally working his way up to being a glorified bagman with future prospects about the same as the past and the present—except for the briefcase tucked under his calves.

The idea was hatched on his last trip to Chicago. Not his idea, but for once Harry Kemp was the main player, the star. He'd be a star for the rest of his life. Go first class. Be a first-rater. He remembered a line from *Julius Caesar*—"There is a tide in the affairs of men, which, taken at the flood, leads on to overwhelming victories."

This was high tide for Harry Kemp.

"What's the matter?" Squeaky broke into the reverie.

"What?"

"I said what's the matter?"

"Nothing's the matter. Why do you ask?"

"Usually you talk. You ain't said nothin' in nearly a hundred miles."

"So?"

"So what's the matter?"

"Nothing's the matter."

"Harry . . ."

"What?"

"I wanna tell you somethin' nobody else knows . . ."

"Look, Squeaky, I'm not a priest. Save it for confession."

"No, it's not like that, Harry—I just made up my mind. This is my last trip."

"What?"

"I'm quittin'."

"All right, you're quitting."

"You see, Harry, I'm sixty-four years of age, nearly sixty-five. I took a lot of shots when I was in the ring, and well, you know, I don't know how much longer I got left before the man counts to ten."

"You'll probably piss on all our graves."

"The thing is Kevin. I told you about my son Kevin, didn't I?"

"Yeah, you told me."

"Well he's got this place up near Newport, Oregon—almost twenty acres. I went up and visited him and his wife Mary Ann last year. They got four kids who call me Pap Pap. Well, Kevin called me up yesterday, and he and Mary Ann want me to go up there and live with them. I told 'em I'd think it over. Harry, you know what I'm going to do?"

"What, Squeaky?"

"When we get to Chicago and take care of business, I'm going to call Kevin and Mary Ann and tell 'em I'm packin' my bags and headin' their way. Ain't that somethin'?"

"Yeah, that's something."

"I guess you're gonna have to find a new partner. We had some good times, didn't we, Harry?"

"Yeah, we did, Squeaky."

"Maybe you'll come up and pay us a visit sometime."

"Maybe I will."

"Bring a raincoat." Squeaky laughed.

Harry looked out of the window at the desolate landscape, grimaced, and rubbed his stomach. "Squeaky, my stomach's killing me. I got to throw up, take a dump—I don't know."

"Jeez, that ain't like you. You're always in good shape."

"Well, I'm not in good shape right now." Harry clawed at his midsection.

"I'll find a gas station."

"Can't wait. I'll puke all over the car. Pull over behind those rocks."

"Yeah, sure."

Squeaky steered the Buick off the paved road onto a

rock-riddled dirt path leading to a bouldered area. After a hundred yards he slowed the car and was about to stop.

"Keep going."

"There's a lot of rocks on this road."

"A little farther. I don't need to have people watching me take a crap."

Squeaky accelerated cautiously and the Buick's underbelly occasionally ground against protruding rocks. He was about to say something when Harry spoke.

"Okay, stop here. I'll be right back."

As the car stopped, Harry opened the door, took the briefcase with him, left the door open, and moved toward a boulder, holding his stomach with his free hand.

"What're you taking the briefcase for?"

"It goes where I go. I said I'll be right back." He disappeared around the rock.

Squeaky sat behind the wheel for ninety seconds, looking at the boulder, then he heard Harry calling with desperation.

"Squeaky, Squeaky, come here quick. Come here!"

Squeaky bolted from the Buick, heeling and toeing toward Harry's voice.

He found Harry bent over, holding his stomach with both hands; the briefcase near his feet.

"Harry, what is it? What's wrong?"

Harry Kemp turned, gun in hand, and fired point-blank between Squeaky's eyes. Squeaky dropped.

"Nothing's wrong," said Harry Kemp.

But Squeaky couldn't hear. To make sure, Harry pointed the gun at the figure on the ground and fired twice into Squeaky Monahan's face.

Chapter 9

Harry Kemp appeared from around the boulder, walking like any other businessman with a briefcase except for the fact that he was tucking a .38 Special revolver back into its holster. Another difference was the contents of the briefcase. Businessmen carry contracts, notes, plans, memos, books, even sandwiches in their briefcases—some carry money, but not this much.

In the Buick, he reloaded the revolver. He didn't think he'd need it again, but just in case. Harry Kemp couldn't resist reaching across to the seat next to him and patting the briefcase. Five million dollars more or less wouldn't make that much difference in the life of Phil Keelo. But the life of Harry Kemp would never be the same. He and his partner would have to disappear from the face of the earth, but that was all set up. With five million dollars you can do a hell of a good disappearing act. This was his day for thinking of quotations, first *Julius Caesar* and now a line from *The Count of Monte Cristo*. He patted the briefcase again and said it out loud. "The world is mine."

He twisted the ignition key, shifted into reverse, backed off the dirt road, turned the car toward the highway, then bolted the Buick back onto the rocky path. There was a piercing noise from under the car, the sound of sharp stone against metal.

The Buick charged from the road onto the highway discharging blue-black oil from its vitals.

A few minutes later, an ominous dark cloud of smoke spewed from the exhaust. It wasn't long before every warning light on the computer panel was flashing while the engine growled complaints as the car commenced to jerk.

"Goddamnsonofabitch!" Harry banged the butt of his fist against the steering wheel and veered off the road.

Holding on to the briefcase, he lifted the hood and looked helplessly at the smoking engine. He didn't know much about automobiles, that was Squeaky's department, but it didn't take a mechanical engineer to determine that this machine was going nowhere unless it was towed or trucked. In frustration Harry kicked the front fender, then walked to the shoulder of the road to hitch a ride.

The oncoming traffic was sparse. Harry waved with his free hand, trying to act as casual as possible and subdue the growing knot of discomfort in the pit of his stomach. He did not welcome any deviation from plan and he had planned every detail. Murder, theft, escape—all planned meticulously. Hitchhiking was not part of the plan.

A truck, a station wagon, and a sedan passed without even slowing down.

The Bronco did slow down, then stopped.

"Got a little trouble, huh?"

"Big trouble. Will you give me a lift?"

Mulligan nodded and waved for Harry to get in. Kemp

opened the door and started to step inside. Mulligan pointed to the disabled Buick.

"Anything you want to take with you from the car?"

"Just this," Harry tapped the briefcase and closed the door. "Can you get me to a car rental agency?"

"Why not?" Mulligan pressed the accelerator pedal and steered the Bronco back onto the road.

"I appreciate this. Can you imagine? A brand-new car. That's the last Buick I'll ever buy."

Mulligan said nothing.

"There's a Hertz in Cedar City—about eighty miles."

"You've got another problem, mister."

A nervous look flashed across Harry's face. His hand edged toward the holstered gun.

"What's that?"

"The air conditioning in this crate's on the fritz."

Harry laughed, a little too loud and a little too long.

Mulligan said nothing for the next ten miles. Harry Kemp started to make small talk a couple of times, but thought better of it. Small talk can lead to questions, and the fewer questions and answers Harry Kemp exchanged with anybody right now, the better.

Artie Lepitino slammed down the hood of the Buick as Ted Sahadi rose from looking at the underbelly of the machine. Their Volvo station wagon was parked just behind the abandoned vehicle.

"Something's screwy, man," Sahadi said. "This car's been abused. Maybe we ought to call Louis."

"Okay, but they've got to be up ahead. We know the stops. We'll catch 'em."

"Suppose they change the route? Change the stops?"

"Why would they do that?"

"I don't know," Sahadi pointed to the Buick. "Why would they do *this?*"

"Come on." Artie Lepitino walked toward the station wagon.

The silence was becoming uncomfortable for Harry Kemp. Mulligan reached into his pocket, pulled out a Montecruz, bit off the end, and lit it with the dashboard lighter.

"I noticed the Utah license plate," Kemp finally said.

Mulligan just nodded and blew out smoke.

"Spend the night in Vegas?"

Mulligan nodded. More smoke.

"Heard there was some excitement there last night."

"Thought there was excitement there every night," Mulligan remarked.

"Not like this. A real old-fashioned shoot-out."

"You don't say. Listen I got to go to the can, stretch my legs—get a nice cold beer." Mulligan pointed to a small cafe just off the road ahead. A faded sign identified it as Flo's.

"Right." Harry nodded. "I'll make a phone call."

Mulligan drove the Bronco off the road onto Flo's parking lot.

Flo's consisted of a counter with four stools, half a dozen small tables, and a booth near the rear. A counter shelf connected the cafe to the kitchen.

Mulligan entered, still smoking the Montecruz. Harry followed, still carrying the briefcase. Mulligan had said that he would lock the Bronco so the briefcase would be safe, but his passenger allowed that he would prefer to take it with him.

Flo, a buxom sixtyish permanent blonde, stood behind the counter chastising in Spanish a Mexican named Bonafacio who was about half Flo's age and weight. Mulligan's Spanish was good enough to get the drift if not the exact translation. Flo's inflection also helped. "You were late again this morning. The place is filthy, you can't even see out of the windows. Listen, Bonafacio, either you get here on time and keep this place decent or I'll get Immigration on your ass. Now start mopping."

Without breaking stride she switched to English and addressed Mulligan and Harry. "Greetings, gents. What's your pleasure?"

"A cold Bud and the men's room." Said Mulligan.

"It's unisex." Flo pointed to the rear. "What'll you have?" she asked Harry.

"Bud Light."

"*Light*, huh." She gave him a disparaging look. "*Dos cervezas, muy frías.*" Flo brought up the beers and set the bottles on the counter, glasses next to them.

Harry picked up the light and a glass, and walked toward the phone on the rear wall near the door to the toilet. Mulligan took a swig from the bottle.

Muy fría." He smiled.

"I purely admire a man who smokes a cigar, 'specially a good cigar," Flo said.

"Care for one?" Mulligan took a Montecruz from his pocket.

"No thanks. Don't use 'em myself."

"Give it to some man you purely admire."

"In that case, *you* keep it."

"In that case, I will." Mulligan took the Bud with him and headed past Harry who was dialing a number on the phone.

On the road outside, Ted pointed from the Volvo toward a sign. "There ought to be a phone in that joint."

Harry Kemp was speaking on the phone, being as casual as he could. "I'll be a little late, so don't leave until I call you. Yeah ... no ... a ..."

Mulligan came out of the toilet, beer bottle in hand, cigar still stuck in his mouth.

"... a good Samaritan named ..." Harry looked at Mulligan. "... Say what *is* your name?"

"Mulligan."

"... Mulligan picked me up. I'll rent a car in Cedar City ..."

Mulligan kept moving. He walked past Bonafacio, who emerged from the kitchen with a mop and pail, and stopped near the big woman who stood behind the counter. Mulligan set down the empty bottle.

"You Flo?"

"Me Flo," she replied. "You Tarzan?"

"Me Mulligan. Me still thirsty."

"Well, shit, Mulligan. We better do something about that." Flo brought up another Bud.

When Artie and Ted entered, Harry had just hung up

and was walking toward the counter with a five dollar bill in one hand and the briefcase in the other.

It was a dead heat as to who was the more surprised and startled—Harry or Ted and Artie. But Artie spoke first.

"Harry!"

"What're you doing here!" Harry Kemp blurted out.

"Where's Squeaky?" Artie looked around, casing the cafe.

"He ... he got sick." Harry stammered. "You tailing us?"

Artie responded by pulling out a gun. Ted did the same.

"Hand over that briefcase," Artie barked.

Harry had already gone for his gun. He ducked behind the counter, where Flo stood, and fired, hitting Artie in the shoulder.

Both Artie and Ted fired back and dove for cover, overturning tables. Ted's table was near the front door. While the wounded Artie shot again at Harry, Ted turned his weapon toward Mulligan, who was crouched by the counter, and saw Ted's leveled gun reflected in the mirror.

Mulligan, cigar still in mouth, spun and flung the beer bottle. It frothed a stream of foam across the room and exploded on Sahadi's forehead. Ted's gun went off, shattering the mirror but missing Mulligan by three feet.

Artie continued his barrage, directed toward Harry. Mulligan crawled behind the counter as Flo rose, bringing up a sawed-off shotgun.

"Eat this, you son of a bitch!" she blared, letting one barrel go, blasting a charge into Artie's chest and face.

Before she could fire the other barrel, Ted, his face leaking blood, shot and hit Flo in the heart.

Harry, holding the briefcase, dashed for the rear door, firing back with his gun hand as he ran. He made it halfway when the bullet struck his spine. Ted fired once more at the fallen man, then peripherally saw Mulligan with the leveled shotgun.

Ted spun to fire, but too late. The impact crashed him into the front wall.

Bonafacio, cowering in a corner, crossed himself.

Harry Kemp was not dead. Not yet.

"Mulligan ... Mulligan ..." He groaned with his penultimate breath.

Mulligan put the shotgun on the counter, picked the stub of the Montecruz off the floor, and took a puff. It was still lit. He walked up to Harry Kemp and leaned close. Kemp tried to say something more, but he failed.

"Mister," Mulligan said, "I never did get your name. But you're a dead man."

He picked up the briefcase and walked, not fast, not slow, toward the entrance. On the way he stepped over Artie's body.

What used to be Ted Sahadi was blocking the door. With his foot, Mulligan rolled him away from the threshold while Bonafacio crossed himself again. Mulligan stooped, picked up Sahadi's 9-mm Beretta, and tucked it into his belt.

Mulligan came out of the cafe entrance, flipped away the butt of the Montecruz, pulled the keys out of his pants pocket, and walked past the Volvo station wagon to his Bronco.

As the Bronco turned onto the roadway, a truck with the lettering ZELLES HAULING pulled into Flo's parking lot and stopped next to the Volvo.

Pete Zelles stepped out of the truck's cab and walked toward the entrance to Flo's. He was a healthy, carefree man of sixty-four, who whistled a tuneless tune, removed the sunglasses from his face, and tucked them into his shirt pocket as he approached the door.

Mulligan turned the Bronco off the roadway onto a picnic area and stopped under the shade of a cedar tree.

Pete Zelles opened the door of the cafe and as usual called out "Hell-low Fl-ow!"

But he did not get the usual response. A thousand times Flo had shouted back, "Pistol Pete, come in and eat!" Not this time.

Pete Zelles viewed the carnage and murmured, "Jesus Christ."

Mulligan popped the latch open with his Uncle Henry knife, lifted the lid of the briefcase, absorbed the sight of the hundred-dollar bills for a moment then exclaimed, "Holy shit!"

Chapter 10

Cedar City Sheriff Frank Mendoza pulled open the long drawer in the morgue room. There was a body in that drawer—and others in the second, the third, the fourth, and the fifth drawers.

The bodies were those of Squeaky Monahan, Flo Baines, Harry Kemp, Ted Sahadi, and Artie Lepitino.

A uniformed deputy stood nearby. So did Johnny Rice and Louis Lepitino. Louis blanched at the sight of his dead brother.

"We're just about out of coolers," Mendoza noted. "Not sure in which order they got it—or who gave it to who." He looked at Louis Lepitino. "That one is your brother, isn't it?"

Lepitino nodded as Johnny Rice stared at him. Mendoza moved toward and pointed at the body of Harry Kemp. "And this one had your hotel on his ID. Work for you, Mr. Rice?"

"Sometimes."

"Uh-huh. What was his line of work?"

"Sort of an accountant."

"What sort of an accountant carries a .38 Special?" Mendoza didn't wait for Rice's answer. He took a step toward Squeaky Monahan's body. "The little one we found behind some rocks near the abandoned Buick. The rest of 'em shot it out at Flo's. More killing in five minutes than there's been here in fifteen years. Never figured for Flo to get it that way. Right through the pump. Either of you know what this was all about?"

"Did your people find a briefcase?" Rice asked.

"Nope. What was in it?"

"Some . . . papers."

"Important?"

Rice did not answer.

"I guess," Mendoza went on, "they were important enough for him to carry a .38 Special and get killed in the bargain. The miracle is that there were two survivors."

"Who?" Rice asked.

"One was a Latino who worked there—illegal. From what we can make out, the other one was named Mulligan."

A half an hour later Johnny Rice and Louis Lepitino were in the rear seat of The Meadows limousine, being driven back to Las Vegas. The divider window was rolled up so the driver could not hear any of the conversation. But there had been no conversation since the limousine left Cedar City. Johnny Rice's face was a thundercloud. Lepitino finally broke the silence.

"Johnny, I swear on my father's grave I didn't know anything about it!"

"If you did, it'll be *your* grave—and maybe mine. You know what's going to happen when I call Chicago?"

"Yeah."

"You see it's like this, Mr. Keelo. First Harry gets ambitious, knocks off Squeaky. Then Artie Lepitino, Louis' young brother, and some outatown cowboy get ambitious..."

"Artie musta gone crazy..."

"And somewhere in this world, Mr. Keelo, there's a guy named Mulligan... with your five million bucks."

Mulligan walked out of the Army Surplus store carrying an unwrapped but rolled-up sleeping bag. He unlocked the Bronco and tossed the sleeping bag on top of the briefcase lying on the passenger side of the floorboard.

Twenty minutes later, at an isolated area, he was stuffing the last of the five million from the briefcase into the sleeping bag. He had set aside a thick stack of bills to use as walking-around money. There was no way to trace them. The money wasn't new. The serial numbers weren't consecutive. Just your basic spendable hundred-dollar bills. In the last twenty-four hours they had already cost five people their lives. They could cost Mulligan his life. But he had risked his life for a lot less—and not just once. Finders keepers, losers weepers. The losers would be coming after him and the money. They'd be coming with guns. But it wouldn't be easy to find him. Mulligan was good at getting lost. And he had a gun too, with a supply of ammunition he had picked up at the surplus store.

* * *

The salesman helped Mulligan load the moped into the bed of the Bronco, then handed him a receipt. "Thank you, Mr. Joseph. I'm sure your nephew will have a lot of fun."

"Yeah, he's a fun-loving kid."

"Make sure he wears the helmet."

"You bet."

Mulligan had found the spot he was looking for. He slipped the gear shift into neutral and let the Bronco idle. He took out what he needed, then went back, lowered the windows, and rammed a board between the front seat and the accelerator. The motor revved hard. In a swift move Mulligan shifted the gear from neutral to drive and jumped away.

The Bronco raced straight ahead, flew off the cliff, seemed suspended for a moment like a wounded bird, then dropped and twisted crazily until it hit into the water a hundred feet below. It did not take long for the Bronco to disappear beneath the gurgling surface.

"Well," Mulligan told himself, "won't have to get the air conditioning fixed."

Mulligan rode the moped back to Tres Cruces. The sleeping bag was rolled up and strapped to the back of the ped. Mulligan wasn't wearing a helmet.

Postal Center
Packaging and Shipping
Mail Boxes—24 hours

Mulligan came out of the door beneath the sign and walked to the parked moped. The sleeping bag had been packaged and shipped.

Next he traded the moped in on a used Camaro and drove northwest.

Chapter 11

Keelo walked naked from the bathroom with the cordless phone in his hand. He was talking over the sound of the running shower. Keelo swung the door as he came through but it didn't quite close. He walked to the bed and sat on its edge.

Johnny Rice sat at his desk and talked into the phone. Louis Lepitino was nearby. So were six persuasive-looking men of assorted sizes and complexions.

"... Mr. Keelo, in the room besides Louis, I've got six of the best men in this part of the country."

"Yeah, what're you going to do? Play poker?"

"We're going to get Mulligan."

"I want my five million."

"When he was at his motel, Mulligan made a phone call to Salt Lake City, to a dame who turns out to be his sister. Name's Ann Robbins."

"So?"

"So that's a start..."

"All I care about is the finish. You fumbled a five-million-dollar ball. You know what the penalty for that is, *Mr. Reizglowiz?*"

"Mr. Keelo—"

"Now you might have good men but you don't have the best. The best is in St. Louis. I'm going to call him so you're gonna have competition. It'd be better for you if *you* came up with the money first."

"I will."

"If somebody gets away with this once, then somebody else is going to get the same idea. That's bad for business."

"Mr. Keelo, you don't have to..." But Keelo had hung up.

"Shit!" Rice slammed the phone onto the cradle. "Keelo's going to call Zable."

Everybody in the room knew the name.

Zable was watching *The Maltese Falcon* on television. It was toward the end of the picture and Bogart was talking to Mary Astor and saying, "... when one of your organization gets killed it's bad business to let the killer get away with it; bad all around."

That was when the phone rang. When Keelo identified himself Zable switched off the set and listened while Keelo filled him in. Zable was a hatchet-faced man with an unfortunate complexion, ice-blue eyes, and an ice-black heart—what there was of it. Soft spoken, but with a razor edge.

"... That's all we know about him," Keelo said.

"That's all I need to know," Zable replied.

"I don't care how many it takes or what it costs—hey, Butterfly, you gonna be in there all night?—find him and get the money back."

"I'll find him—and the money." It was Zable who hung up the phone.

Mulligan stood in the phone booth with stacks of quarters in front of him.

"... Where are you calling from, Mr. Mulligan," Annie asked, "or is that privileged information?"

"Never mind that. Listen, Annie, I got the pot of gold—not a pot, a barrel. And it's stashed at the end of a rainbow."

"You make as much sense as usual."

"Quit cracking wise ..."

"... No more cracking."

"Here's what I want you to do. In my closet get the what-Claire-doesn't know shoe box—there should be over two thousand bucks—"

"... Closer to three."

"Good."

"What do you want me to do with it?"

"Take a vacation."

"What?"

"You've always wanted to see Hawaii—see it. Stay at least a month. The Royal Lahaina in Maui is a good hotel."

"I have to make arrangements at the library ..."

"Make 'em. What the hell, you own the joint."

"No I don't *own* the joint."

"Quit if you have to."

"Mulligan . . ."

"If anybody asks—*anybody*, including Bernard—you haven't heard from me since Vegas."

"Mulligan, you remember 'The Rime of the Ancient Mariner'?"

"No."

"Yes you do—'Like one, that on a lonesome road doth walk in fear and dread, and having once turned round walks on, and turns no more his head, because he knows, a frightful fiend doth close behind him tread.' "

"So?"

"So how many fiends you got on your ass?"

"No more than usual. You watching Carson?"

"It's a rerun. I'm paying bills . . ."

"When you get back you'll never have to worry about paying bills or anything else."

"In Vegas, don't tell me you gambled."

"Sort off."

"You are a crazy sonofabitch, but *sé agapo*—that's Greek for I love you, remember?"

"Yeah, I remember. See you, kid."

"Sure." Annie hung up the phone.

That was about as close as Mulligan had ever come to saying good-bye to her. There were a lot of things Mulligan didn't say, or have to say. Annie knew how much he loved her, protected her; from the time she could remember. Even though he was a year younger, he was streetwise and tough. Nobody messed around with Mulligan's sister.

There was the time Annie had a date with Bob Cousino. She wasn't quite eighteen. Cousino was nineteen and went around saying that he was French and passionate. He tried to get passionate with Annie in the car parked near the Mulligans' house on Lagrange Street. Cousino had unbuttoned her blouse and, against her struggling, was working on her skirt when Mulligan pulled the door open, lifted Cousino out of the car, tore the shirt off his back, and kicked him in the balls. He escorted Annie to the front door then drove to the C.P.S.A., a private upstairs club on the corner of Erie and Bush where they served beer to minors, at least to Mulligan.

Mulligan's father was a cop. For over twenty years he foot patrolled the area of Summit and Cherry Streets, Toledo's Skid Row. In the late twenties and early thirties that had been the battleground of the Prohibition gang wars between Yonnie Licavoli and Jack Kennedy. Licavoli had told Scarface Al Capone to "stay the fuck out of Toledo." Capone stayed out. Kennedy declared himself in. Twenty-four-year-old Jack Kennedy was shot and killed by the Licavoli mob the day Sean Mulligan became a rookie. Still there were times when Sean Mulligan played follow the bleeder, after firing his police special into hijackers, bank robbers, burglars, and injudicious gamblers.

Sean Mulligan married a girl from Greece, Eurydice Theopoulos, and for the first few years their two kids spoke more Greek than English around the house on Lagrange Street.

Sean Mulligan had many opportunities for promotion and advancement to a better and safer beat. He took the promotions, became a sergeant, but wouldn't give up his beat.

Though she never let it show, Eurydice Mulligan lived in daily and nightly dread that her husband would be shot or killed around Summit and Cherry.

Instead, Sean and Eurydice Mulligan both were killed in an automobile accident on the Dixie Highway, coming back from Detroit, when a drunk driver crossed the line and hit them head-on. It was Mulligan who took charge, saw to it that Annie graduated from Toledo University, then got her master's degree from Ohio State, where she wrote her thesis on Thorton Wilder's *The Skin of Our Teeth*.

When she met and fell in love with Tom Robbins, who called her 'Bright Eyes,' Mulligan couldn't have been happier. Robbins was almost as tough as Mulligan, but completely different; outgoing, smiling, talking, quoting poetry to Annie, dancing with her—always requesting their favorite song, "Dancing in the Dark," and singing it to her while he held her tenderly close. They settled in Salt Lake City, where Tom worked for an airline.

And when Mulligan found out he was going to be an uncle he lit up like the High Level Bridge. Robbins was already in Vietnam, and Mulligan and Browne were on their way. Robbins and Mulligan met up in Saigon and compared pictures of a very pregnant Annie.

Tom had a premonition. All soldiers do. He managed to call her twice and wrote letters every day, filled with suggestions for boys' and girls' names. "Dear Bright Eyes, Whatever it is," he wrote, "we'll have one of the opposite sex next year."

It was a boy. Born dead. But Tom Robbins never knew. He had been dead for eight days. Mulligan tried to keep it from Annie, but she found out the day before she went into the hospital.

Now Annie picked up the mug of tea from the desk and walked to the bed stand. She looked at the picture—her and Tom Robbins. It was taken less than a week after the doctor confirmed that she was pregnant. They hadn't told anybody yet, but there was that I've-got-a-secret smile on both their faces as he held her close and tenderly.

She never slept with another man. After a few years when Mulligan married Claire, a marriage Annie knew was made in hell, she dated, but it was hopeless. Annie could never erase the memory of Tom's face, the sound of his voice, the touch of his hand, or the feel of his body. Nor did she want to.

She endured the misery of Mulligan's marriage, knowing her brother was risking his life on assignments for Keyes only to come home and do battle with Claire in a war at which he was less skilled and practiced.

Finally Mulligan moved into the spare room in Annie's little house, and Claire disappeared with just about all of his cash. But Mulligan had found her, just as Annie knew he would. Mulligan was a natural hunter when he himself wasn't being hunted.

From the sound of his voice, knowing him as she did, Annie had the feeling that he was being hunted now. But his voice had no fear in it. Curiously, it was much more alive, alert, and in control than it had been for a long time.

Whatever it was, she didn't think it had to do with Keyes. There were no barrels of gold at the end of any of Keyes's rainbows.

And it probably didn't have anything to do with Claire. That left Las Vegas.

Louis Lepitino couldn't sleep. He was not a drinker, but he poured two tumblers of Stolichnaya from the bottle and drank them like soda pop. All that did was bring the image of his brother's perforated face and chest into clearer focus.

When he had called his mother and told her he was shipping Artie's body home to be buried next to his father, she became hysterical and almost fainted. Louis promised to be there for the funeral. Luckily, Louis' sister was at home to calm their mother down. Then she got on the phone, said, "Louis, you're a no-good asshole—always were, always will be," and hung up.

Louis knew that he had stepped out of his league and stumbled. Artie and Ted Sahadi took the fall. But if Keelo or Rice or anybody found out that it was his idea, the remains of Louis Lepitino would be relegated to the same mysterious realm occupied by Jimmy Hoffa and hundreds of others who had vanished off the surface of the earth's soil and sea.

Mulligan couldn't know. It wasn't likely he and Artie and Sahadi had talked things over during their brief encounter at Flo's, or that Artie had offered to cut Mulligan in on the heist. Things happened too fast. Especially for Artie and Ted. They were *really* out of their league. But neither they nor Louis could have foretold that Harry Kemp would pick this run to double-cross Keelo and Rice. And now Keelo had called in Zable. Louis had to stick close by. His sister was right, he was a no-good asshole. He had no intention of going home for Artie's funeral. His intention was to look out for number one.

It behooved Lepitino to do everything he could to help Rice get back the five million before Zable did. That way Rice would make points with Keelo—and Lepitino would make points with Johnny Rice. And that would add to the chances of his staying alive, even though he had ended up with pockets full of empty.

It also behooved Lepitino to get some sleep. Rice had invited Detective-Lieutenant Bernard Browne to come and have breakfast in just a few hours. Lepitino was expected to be there. There was one thing that always made him relax and sleep.

Louis Lepitino dialed the number of his favorite whore.

Mulligan had decided to wait until morning to call Keyes. Keyes would be surprised to hear from him. But how many times had Keyes surprised Mulligan? Even from the first time they met. Keyes was the blandest, most nondescript man Mulligan could recall—or not recall. They had spent half an hour together during that first meeting, and twenty minutes later Mulligan would have been hard put to describe him. Someone once said "Keyes's own father couldn't pick him out of a roomful of Rotarians."

While Keyes's appearance was bland, his mind was not. His schemes, subterfuges, and machinations would have made Machiavelli muse. His mind was not only mathematical, but methodical, imaginative, and unscrupulous, except when it came to loyalty to his job. He answered to no one except the Director, and sometimes even those answers were . . . vague. Only because Keyes intended them to be.

Eight Directors had come and gone. Keyes stayed. Two presidents, a Republican and a Democrat, had offered the top job to Keyes. Keyes declined.

In any other profession, Keyes might have become a

multimillionaire. Instead he opted to affect the course of history—anonymously.

He headed TASK FORCE ELEVEN, so called because the eleventh letter of the alphabet is K—for Keyes. His budget was as unlimited as his audacity. And for the most audacious assignments, more often than not Keyes would call in Mulligan. Tomorrow Mulligan would call Keyes, but that night as he lay in the mom-and-pop motel room, he remembered a brainchild of Keyes that was called OPERATION HITCH, *called* because no report was ever put on paper, no detail ever written. OPERATION HITCH made the affair at Flo's seem like a lovers' spat.

In 1976 Colonel Muammar El-Qaddafi was the conquering hero of Libya. In 1969 he had deposed the monarchy of King Idris, taken command of the country, and imposed maniacal rule that included worldwide terrorism and a pledge to destroy all enemies of his nation. In the mid 1970s, the one particular enemy he had in mind was Egypt, his neighbor to the immediate east, ruled by Anwar el-Sadat.

Backed by billions of dollars from his oil-soaked country, Qaddafi went on a buying binge. But the items on his shopping list could not be found in any supermarket, department store, or hardware store. Through his cousin, Sayed Qaddafadam, who was in charge of acquisitions, Qaddafi spent some of those billions on such diverse items as surveillance systems, time-delay detonators, Triex and Quadrex, aluminum stearate to be used for napalm, a fleet of C-130 cargo transports, CH-47 Chinook cargo- and troop- carrying helicopters, smoke grenades, mortar tubes and shells, thousands of M-16 automatic rifles, and millions of rounds of ammunition. But the blue-ribbon item on the list was tons of C-4.

C-4 was a mixture of RDX, the most devastating non-nuclear explosive on the planet, and a chemical compound that rendered it binding. Put them both together and they added up to Plastique, the terrorists' favorite toy. With the proper timing device, it could go off in seconds or next season.

All this firepower was sent to and stored at a secret base near Benghazi and not that far from Qaddafi's immediate neighbor to the east, Anwar el-Sadat's Egypt.

The purchases were being made through a Syrian-born American citizen named Philip Mansour.

What neither Qaddafi, nor his acquisitive cousin knew, or suspected was that Philip Mansour was a part of TASK FORCE ELEVEN, working under direct orders from Keyes and placing hundreds of millions of profit dollars into the coffers of TASK FORCE ELEVEN.

All the arms and explosives were in usable if not first-class condition. They had to be inspected before Qaddafi would pay off. But there was another element included in the deal. Philip Mansour would provide a team of seven men, a high-powered attack and demolition unit, to instruct the Libyans in the art of attack and demolition, ex-Vietnam veterans who were now in it for the love of money instead of country. Mercenaries.

Another thing neither Qaddafi, nor Qaddafadam knew was that the team being provided by Mansour was provided to him by Keyes. The team leader, Don Higley, had been wounded in Vietnam and later dishonorably discharged, having been accused, but not convicted, of stealing arms and equipment that ended up on the wrong side in the "Secret War" across the Laotian border.

Higley had been wounded but not discharged, and he did not deal arms to the enemy. "Higley" was Mulligan—with fake papers, passport, and even a fake birthmark. The other six were ex–Green Berets, all of whom had previously worked undercover with Mulligan-Higley.

They were to receive fifty thousand dollars apiece from the Libyans for three months' work, half paid in advance in cash before their arrival. Higley's deal was a little sweeter. Seventy-five thousand. Loose change for Qaddafi.

Upon their arrival, the seven were greeted by another cousin of Qaddafi's named Alkazar, ushered past immigration without pause. Wined, dined, and womaned that night in Tripoli, they were then flown to the Benghazi base in a recently purchased C-130.

The mercenaries, under Higley's command, commenced instructing the Libyan commando-terrorists, but they also did a little moonlighting. Meanwhile, Qaddafi's anti-Sadat rhetoric reached fever pitch. In addition to the rhetoric, Qaddafi sent units across the border to provoke the Egyptians into retaliatory action, giving Qaddafi occasion to employ some of the material and men in which he had invested.

An armed conflict leading to war was inevitable—except for OPERATION HITCH. Yes, the Higley mercenaries were teaching the art of assassination and sabotage, but they were also doing some sabotaging themselves. While the students were becoming proficient in the methodology of murder and the art of deploying C-4 into innocent objects such as radios, automobiles, telephones, walking sticks, projectors, packages, bridges, bonbons, railroad tracks and bedposts, their teachers had deployed enough C-4 in strategic recesses of the base to blow up a city.

The Lybyans were on alert. The invasion was imminent. So was OPERATION HITCH.

The cool desert night heated up fast. A series of progressively more powerful explosions blasted through the base.

The supply warehouse went first, then the transportation depot, the airplane hangars, the fleet of C-130 cargo carriers, the rifle and ammunition storehouse, the bomb factory, the radar units, and the caravan of CH-47 helicopters—all but one. That one lifted gently into the night, away from the holocaust, carrying seven smiling men who had carried out OPERATION HITCH without a hitch.

Two hours later the CH-47 set down at first light of dawn on a Greek freighter, under Panamanian registry and owned and operated by TASK FORCE ELEVEN, which was later sold by Keyes for an obscene profit.

Not a bad night's work. Keyes, Mulligan, and company had sold Qaddafi billions of dollars worth of marginal arms and equipment at a double markup of the market price, then had destroyed it and, in the process, defused a war. Qaddafi made sure that the world never heard about the incident, saving himself embarrassment and humiliation. But Sadat heard about it. Keyes made sure of that.

For leading the miniexpeditionary force, Mulligan added the fourth Distinquished Intelligence Medal to his collection. The DIM is the highest honor bestowed by the Company.

Mulligan smiled in the bed of the mom-and-pop motel. He would get no medal for the incident at Flo's. But he had something better. Five million dollars. If he stayed alive.

Chapter 12

Rice's penthouse garden overlooked three hundred sixty degrees of Las Vegas hotels, motels, swimming pools, golf courses, streets and desert.

An airplane passed overhead, coming in eastward from San Diego, with a human cargo of winners. Another crossed at a lower altitude, westward, leaving McCarran for Los Angeles with a shipment of losers.

Hector, Johnny Rice's houseman filled the coffee cups for the third time for Rice, Lepitino, and Browne.

"Well, Mr. Rice, we've talked about the weather," Browne observed, "my wound, the new shows in town—and everything except how ducks make love and what we're really here to talk about."

"There is something I wanted to mention." Rice smiled.

"Mention it. Maybe it's even something about the recent unpleasantness near Cedar City." Browne looked at Lepitino. "I'm sorry about your brother."

"Yeah, Artie went a little haywire, if I'd known he had anything like that in mind I'd—"

"Anything like *what?*" Browne asked.

Lepitino didn't know how to answer. He glanced at Rice. Before either Lepitino or Rice spoke, Browne went on. "You mean that he'd get involved in a gunfight? You knew he carried a gun. So did I. He had a permit. What went down at Flo's, Louis? What was all that shooting about?"

"I don't know," Lepitino shrugged. "And it's out of your jurisdiction, isn't it, Lieutenant?"

"My jurisdiction is sometimes . . . flexible."

"Let's all take it easy." Rice smiled some more. "Lieutenant, there's something peculiar here. Very peculiar."

"Such as?"

"Such as for years we've been getting along very nicely. No trouble. We make your job easier when we can, and you—"

"Do my job."

"Yeah, like in the Albert situation. Peaches and cream. Wine and roses."

Browne took a bite of his breakfast and held up the fork. "Ham and eggs."

"Yeah," Lepitino's voice took on a grimmer tone. "And maybe like you and your friend Mulligan."

"What about Mulligan?"

"I don't know. Tell me about him."

"He's got a hangman's knot for a heart, and he can spit icicles in hell. Anything else you want to know about him?"

"That's up to you."

"Then that's all there is."

"Except all of a sudden when your friend shows up there's gunplay."

"Coincidence, but I'm glad because he saved my ass."

"That part's good." Rice nodded. "But then a few miles out of town he gets himself involved in more gunplay. Bodies droppin' like ripe fruit. And your friend Mulligan gets away with ..."

"With *what?*"

Rice shrugged. "Something that don't belong to him. That part's not good. You know?"

"I know that you know a lot more about what happened than I know. But I do know this: whatever happened, Mulligan didn't plan it. He wasn't carrying a gun."

"Yeah, well right now there's people looking for him—and they *are* carrying guns."

"So were Harry and Artie. Mulligan must not have noticed."

"Oh, he's gonna take notice, all right. But he's your friend, and you've got to live in this town, don't you?"

"What're you dealing, Johnny?"

"Just this. Talk to him—and talk sense."

"If I could talk to him I wouldn't even know what the hell to talk about, would I?"

"*He* knows. A lot of things can be overlooked, under the right circumstances. It'd be better if he came back and talked to me, or I'll meet him someplace. We can forget all about what happened." Rice looked at Lepitino. "Except we're sorry for what happened to Louis' brother. But life goes on, don't it, Lieutenant?"

Browne finished his coffee, dabbed his mouth with the linen napkin and rose.

"Get this, Mr. Rice. Anybody breaks the law in this town—you, Mulligan, or a tourist from Toledo—I'm gonna do my job. I don't give a shit what you're dealing."

Lepitino also stood.

Browne pulled out a fold of money and placed a ten dollar bill near his plate.

"That ought to cover the ham and eggs." He started to walk. Lepitino stepped out of his way, but Browne paused for a moment and added, "I've heard that when ducks make love, they think of swans."

The President of the United States and less than one hundred other people in the world knew the coded number that could be dialed directly from almost any part of the "Free World" and some parts of the not so free world. Mulligan dialed.

One of two people would answer. Keyes or Miss Fetzer.

"Hello." The voice was not Keyes's.

Frances Fetzer was present the first time Mulligan walked in to see Keyes. She had been there since he formed TASK FORCE ELEVEN. She favored tailored suits and they favored her. If the suits were an attempt to camouflage the spheres of her figure, it was the only thing in which Miss Fetzer failed. But Miss Fetzer's figure did not consist solely of spheres. She was tall, tall as Keyes. She had long, slender but strong hands, with complementary legs. Miss Fetzer's complexion was Californian, rather than Washingtonian, and it set off classic features except for lips that some women covetously remarked were too large and too red. She wore little or no make-up except for a touch of lipstick from a tube that lasted a long time. Her eyes were emerald green and lucent, her hair the color of burnished copper. Her age was indeterminate, maybe early forties but she looked younger. Nobody, including

Keyes, ever called her anything but Miss Fetzer—not Ms., Miss Fetzer.

The sole exception was during the only intimate weekend she and Mulligan ever spent together. It was a long time coming. Until then they had not so much as touched each other's hands.

Early one Friday autumn evening they both left Keyes's office and entered the empty elevator. As it started to descend she looked at him and said almost matter-of-factly, "Mulligan, let's get it out of our systems."

As the elevator went down a flush went up Mulligan's body. It started in the nether regions and finally exploded in his brain.

"You mean it?"

"Come with me."

Neither said another word. In the parking garage they got into her car and she drove directly to a hotel miles away overlooking the bay. If the clerk or any of the other personnel had ever seen her before, then they were better actors than those who currently performed on television.

He called room service and she walked toward the bathroom. In less than five minutes Mulligan took delivery of a bottle of Glenfiddich and a tray containing two glasses and a bowl of ice. He poured the scotch into cubed glasses, placed them in the palm of his large hand, walked to the bathroom door, and knocked just as the shower went off.

"Come." It was the first word between them since the elevator.

Her body glistened as she stepped, wet and fresh as a spring garden, from the stall. Everything was ripe, from meadowland to hillocks. Mulligan marvelled at the sight.

"On the rocks?" He held out a glass.

She took it and a sip, then handed him a towel.

"Dry me." She turned her back to him.

He set down his glass, then gently patted her gleaming body: arms, shoulders, and waist. She turned to face him again and her soft and ready breasts brushed the rough knuckles of his right hand.

"That's dry enough." She placed her glass on the sink and started by unbuttoning his shirt and continued until they were both naked.

She meshed into his arms and pressed her smooth and tender lips onto his mouth. The flush hit Mulligan again. Harder.

"Miss Fetzer," he murmured.

"Call me Frances."

Mulligan lifted Frances, carried her through the door and onto the bed.

Mulligan was a man of the world who had been with many women all over the world. Women of varying hues, dimensions, and preferences. Some were kittens, some were cats, and some were tigers. Some were shy and some were bold. Some were hot and some were cold. Some were sweet and some were savage. Some were tough and some were tender.

Frances Fetzer was all of this and more. After the first explosive but exploratory encounter, they took their time, time after time, until no more exploration was necessary. Each gave and received and came to know every corner and crevice, every curve and column, every quay and quirk of the other's mind and body.

There was no Keyes or Company, no sabotage or assassination, no cover or covert operation.

They stayed there until Monday's dawn.

She drove him back to his apartment in Washington. Before he left the car he leaned close to kiss her.

"Frances ..."

"Call me Miss Fetzer," she said.

Mulligan knew that it was over. The first and last—the only—time they'd be together like that. Maybe she was too dedicated to Keyes and the work they were doing. Maybe she didn't relish the prospect of getting deeply involved with a spook who could get killed on the next assignment, or even between assignments.

Maybe it was as she had said, "something they had to get out of their systems." Whatever it was, it was over, but at least it happened.

Mulligan stepped out of the car and closed the door. The car immediately pulled away.

Miss Fetzer never looked back.

"Hello," Miss Fetzer repeated.

"This is Argonaut." Of course Keyes had known that Mulligan's mother was Greek. He assigned Mulligan the code name Argonaut and never changed it. "Is Keyes there?"

Neither Keyes nor Miss Fetzer ever wasted words or indulged in preliminaries. Their time was too precious. Mulligan's time wasn't all that precious, but whenever he spoke to Keyes or Miss Fetzer he aborted preliminaries and got straight to the point, sans small talk.

"Mr. Keyes is away until Friday." Efficient. Businesslike.

"Can he be reached?"

"Mr. Keyes is vacationing. Is this an emergency?" She might as well have asked what the weather was like.

Keyes hadn't taken a day's vacation in twenty years. "Vacation" was code for "out of the city or country," possibly with some Third World leader, some second-rate dictator, or at Camp David briefing the "Leading Man" as the President was coded, ironically long before Ronald Reagan succeeded several other "Leading Men" and since the current "Leading Man" succeeded him. Keyes didn't just brief Presidents, he helped shape policy.

Waiting until Friday would be dangerous for Mulligan, but he needed Keyes to personally make a delivery. It would be unwise to interrupt Keyes's official business in order to cash a marker for Mulligan who didn't amount to a hill of beans in the overall scheme of things. Mulligan decided in an instant.

"Only a minor emergency. It can wait until Friday."

"Is there a number Mr. Keyes can call?"

"I'll call him." Mulligan hung up. Damn her cold ass, he thought, but immediately thought better. Miss Fetzer was one of the best things that ever happened to Keyes—and to the Company.

Mulligan couldn't help wondering if Keyes and Miss Fetzer ever "got it out of their systems."

If Mulligan had been a betting man, he would have bet against it.

Chapter 13

Ever since his breakfast sparring match with Rice, who had Lepitino and God knows how many other goons in his corner, while the lieutenant had only his badge and gun, Browne had been trying to reach Annie in order to reach Mulligan.

He did not make the calls from headquarters. First he stopped at a pay phone. There was no answer at Annie's house. He called the library where she was in charge. Mrs. Robbins has just left. No, the lady who answered did not know Mrs. Robbins' destination. Browne tried the house number again, still no answer. He headed for headquarters, went through the motions for over an hour, ducked out "to pick up a pair of shoes from the repair shop." He did do that. Browne also placed another call. Annie was still out. Back to headquarters. He would call again during his lunch hour.

About ten minutes before he intended to break for lunch, the phone rang. Detective Joe Rodriguez reached over, picked it up, and said, "Rodriguez."

He listened for a moment, smiled, and nodded. "Yes,

he's here." Rodriguez covered the mouthpiece. "It's for you. Guess who?"

"The captain?"

"You lose. Actually you win."

"Games, he's playing. Games." Browne took the phone. "Hello."

"Hello, Brownie, I hear you cheated while I was away. Went out with Mulligan."

"Louise, when did you get back?"

"About an hour ago. I go away for a few days and you go and get your head ventilated. How do you feel?"

"Fine. Are you at the agency?"

"No, I'm home. But I called in and they told me about it. Why don't you come by, pick me up, and we'll go have lunch at one of the cop stops?"

"I'll come over, but let's just fix a sandwich there."

"You want to use the 'you know what' again. Well I guess this qualifies as a cop stop, but only for a certain cop."

"Louise . . ."

"Maybe you can even take a quick dip . . . in the pool."

"Louise . . ."

"I'll lay out your bathing suit. 'Bye, Brownie."

Browne hung up the phone. "Joe, I regret to inform you I will not be lunching with you this day."

"So I gathered, you lucky dog."

Browne reached for the door as Rodriguez added. "I brown-bagged it—so there!"

"I might be a little late," the lieutenant said from the doorway.

"You're nuts if you're not."

* * *

Louise lived in a house on a hill fifteen minutes from the Strip. She paid a million dollars cash when she bought it. It was now worth two million. But that was the story of Louise Mundy's life, at least the last fifteen years of it. Born on a hard-scrabble Arkansas farm, left home at fifteen, married in New York at sixteen. Her husband dealt dope and used it. He tried to hook her but didn't. She left him on her eighteenth birthday, went to night school and modeled. Graduated from NYU four years later, when she had become the highest-paid black model in the city. With the money she saved she bought a travel agency that was on the threshold of bankruptcy. But, because of Louise Mundy, the agency never crossed that threshold.

Six years later she sold the business for a million-dollar profit, moved to Las Vegas, where she was going to retire because she liked the desert climate; but after nine months, she opened another travel agency and further prospered.

One night she shot and critically wounded a man who broke and entered with rape in mind. Detective-Lieutenant Bernard Browne answered the call and that's how it began. She was the only one he ever let call him Brownie.

She answered the door herself and kissed him.

"Where's Sam and Candida?" he asked.

"I gave them the rest of the day off. You sure you're okay?"

He nodded and looked at her. Louise Mundy could still model if she wanted to. If she had put on ten pounds they were all in the right places. And her face was still flawless.

"Miss me?" She smiled.

'You'll find out."

"I certainly hope so. Just for the record," she added, "let me ask you one more time. Will you marry me?"

"It seems to me I've already answered that question one or two thousand times. Something like this—so I can become accustomed to living like this? Or so you can become accustomed to living on a cop's salary? P.S. I love you, Louise."

"Brownie, you're playing a dangerous game. I just might call this whole thing off in ten or twenty years—but first I'll fix that sandwich."

"I got to make a call."

"Figured that out all by myself. You think the captain is bugging your line?"

"No, but it's not police business. By the way it's a toll call."

"I'll see that you pay," she smiled again, "one way or another," and went into another room.

This time Annie answered on the living-room phone.

"Annie, this is Bernard."

"How's the bumper?"

"The what?"

"Your head. Mulligan told me you needed a little repair work."

"My head's fine. I'm not so sure about his."

"Bernie, what's happened? Is he hurt?"

"No, I don't think so. But I've got to find him, talk to him. Where is he?"

"I don't know."

"Annie, he must have called you ..."

"No. I don't know where he is, and I haven't heard from him since that night in Vegas."

"Right. That's what he told you to say and you said it. But, Annie, they're after his ass, coming from all directions!"

"Sorry . . ."

"This is me! I'm trying to help."

"Don't you think I know that? There's nothing I can tell you."

"I understand. If you hear from him, tell him to call. Important. And, Annie, I think it's a good idea for you to take a trip somewhere."

"Know what, Bernard? I was about to start packing for Hawaii."

A knock came from the front door. Annie looked in that direction. "Matter of fact, I believe the airline ticket is just being delivered. *Aloha, Bernard.*"

"*Aloha,*" said a resigned Bernard Browne, and he hung up the phone as Louise entered the room.

"Did you get through okay?"

"Sort of. Where's lunch?"

"In the kitchen, but let's take that dip first."

"Okay." He looked around. "I thought you were going to lay out my trunks."

"You won't need them." Louise Mundy smiled.

As Annie hung up and started walking toward the front door there was another, slightly more persistent knock.

"Yes, I'm coming."

The door had a chain latch. Without unlatching it, Annie opened the door as far as the chain would allow, about three inches. "Are you from—"

The door burst open violently, snapping the latch like a candy cane. A big man had kicked it open. He walked in two steps and, as Annie tried to draw back, grabbed her in an agonizing grip, his thick arm across her chest, pinning both of her arms. His other hawser hand slammed roughly over her mouth and nose, so she could not speak and could just barely breathe.

A hatchet-faced man with an unfortunate complexion entered the room and closed the door quietly.

"Ease up a little, Crago." Zable spoke softly but with that edge. He sounded as if he were doing an imitation of Jack Palance. Crago eased up a little so she could breathe slightly better, but still did not speak.

"We're just here to ask you a question. We don't want to hurt you. Now when I ask you that question," Zable looked at Crago, "he's going to take his hand away. Don't scream. Just answer the question. You will be tied up so you can free yourself in just a few minutes after we leave." He nodded toward Crago, then spoke to Annie. "Where is he?"

Crago removed his hand from her mouth, but kept it close to her face. His other arm still held her firmly and moved rudely across her breasts.

"Where?" Zable repeated.

"Where's who?"

By now Crago had cupped his hand around her right breast and began to massage with his stubby fingers.

"Tell us," Zable said, "and tell us fast—where is your brother?"

"First you tell this ape to quit."

Zable nodded. "Crago." Crago's fingers stopped moving but stayed cupped.

"I don't know where he is."

"Let me explain, and only once. We don't want to hurt you or your brother. But he's got something that doesn't belong to him. It's our job to get it back where it belongs. Now where is he?"

"I don't know—"

Zable viciously backhanded Annie's face. Her head bounced crazily against Crago's shoulder. An axe blade of pain chopped into her brain. Blood leaked from her mouth and nose. Her nose had been broken.

Zable jabbed a long pointed finger hard against the nostril of her bleeding nose.

"You are an attractive woman. This is your last chance to stay that way. Where?"

Annie nodded and swallowed as if she were about to answer the question, then said, "Fuck you!"

Zable's fist crashed into her left eye and cheek, breaking skin. But he knew his business. He hadn't hit her hard enough to make her lose consciousness.

"Where?"

"I don't ...," Annie breathed deeply and girded for more, " ... don't know."

It came. Zable's knuckles burst into her rib cage. She bled more and now was barely conscious. She choked, grasping for air.

"I swear ... I ... don't know."

Zable said nothing for almost a minute, letting her gather strength as Crago still held her on her feet.

He finally spoke. "Let her go."

Crago slowly took his hands off her. Annie swayed, trying to maintain her balance. Her face was now swollen and discolored. Blood from her cheek and nose ran down her throat onto her blouse. Even through her unhurt eye, all she could see was a hazy shadow.

From under his jacket, Zable removed a revolver fitted

with a silencer. Crago took a step away from her. Zable aimed the revolver at her heart. Annie barely realized what was happening and was powerless to stop it.

As he fired she said one word.

It might have been "don't" or it might have been "Tom." The word was swallowed by the pop of the bullet that hit her heart.

She fell, twisting against an end table, and slumped dead onto the floor.

Zable unfitted the silencer, put it into a pocket, and replaced the gun under his jacket.

Crago looked down at the body. "I don't think she knew."

"She didn't."

"Then," he shrugged, "what good did this do?"

Zable reached down and tore off her blouse. He proceeded to remove her clothes until he had stripped her naked, then he replied.

"Mulligan and his sister were close. Very close. This way maybe we don't have to go looking for him. Maybe he'll come looking for us."

Crago smiled and studied the naked body. "She sure was a good-looking woman."

"Yeah," Zable agreed. "Hand me the rope."

"She's already dead. What're you gonna do with the rope?"

"I'm gonna hang her."

Chapter 14

As usual Mulligan awoke early. He shaved, showered, and collected the fishing gear he had bought the day before, after Miss Fetzer informed him that Keyes would not be back until Friday.

He was heading toward the Camaro, when he heard Pop's voice. "Mr. Joseph, good morning."

"Morning."

"Everything okay? Sleep all right?"

"First-rate."

"Air conditioning working okay?"

"Works fine."

"Gonna be hot today."

"Looks like."

"Have any idea how long you're going to be with us? Just wondering."

Mulligan held up the tackle box as he opened the car door. "Not sure. Depends on how smart the fish are."

"If you're going to Loon Lake, work off the south shore, that's where all the dumb fish hang out."

"Thanks for the tip. Going to get some breakfast first."

"Cousin Ernie's got a little joint on the corner of Main and Fifth. Good eats. Can't miss it. Called Ernie's."

"Thanks for that tip too."

Mulligan drove off toward Tres Cruces.

He parked the Camaro on Main Street and was heading for Ernie's when he saw the newsstand with the sign OUT OF TOWN NEWSPAPERS across the street. That made sense. It was unlikely that Tres Cruces published a local newspaper. Maybe a weekly, or monthly.

Mulligan walked across the street and greeted the old lady who ran the stand.

"Morning," she replied through a smile, revealing a missing upper plate.

"Got a Salt Lake City paper, ma'am?"

"*Journal.*" She nodded, and selected a paper from the stand. "Fresh off the press, yesterday."

"Good enough."

Mulligan paid for the paper and gave her a quarter tip. He walked back across the street and went into Ernie's for some good eats.

Ernie himself was behind the short-order stove, and the lady near the cash register had to be Mrs. Ernie. Tres Cruces, it appeared, was a mom-and-pop town.

As he sat at the counter, Mrs. Ernie was already pouring his coffee.

"What'll you have, mister?"

"Just some rye toast and marmalade if you've got it, no butter."

"We got it. Ought to have some scrambled eggs, real fresh."

"Okay."

"And a nice slice of fresh ham."

"Right." Mulligan sipped the black coffee and started to look at the paper.

"Stayin' at Mom and Pop's?"

"Right."

"They send you here?"

"Pop did."

"Uh-huh. Gonna be here long?"

"Long enough to do a little fishing."

"Loon Lake?"

"Right."

"Fish on the east shore. That's where they bite."

"Thanks for the tip." Mulligan drank more coffee and went back to the paper as Mrs. Ernie walked toward Ernie himself.

The story was on the front page, just below the fold, two columns, bylined Norman Wolfe.

BIZARRE MURDER BAFFLES POLICE

The naked body of Ann Robbins who had been shot in the heart and then hanged in her own home was found this afternoon by Herbert Cloud who was delivering an airline ticket. The victim had been beaten about the face and body. Captain Sven Olsen of the Salt Lake City Homicide Division refused to divulge whether the police had any clues, motive, or suspect ...

Mulligan managed to set the cup on the counter as the image of what he had just read burned into his brain.

Annie. Beaten. Shot. Hanged. Annie.

How many times before and during combat, and during the dirty, deadly work he did for Keyes in hot spots all over the world, did he imagine the time when his sister Annie would receive word of his death? How many times did he say goodbye to her without actually saying it?

How many times did he wonder if they'd ship his body back to her—and what shape it would be in if it ever got there? Not that it really mattered. Dead is dead.

And now here he was, alive in some no-place flyspeck reading that Annie was dead.

Annie. Beaten. Shot. Hanged. Annie.

Mulligan did not know how long he sat there, but the sight of the scrambled eggs and the slice of ham on the plate being set on the counter almost made him vomit.

"You all right, mister?" the woman asked. "Something wrong?"

Mulligan rose, placed a five dollar bill on the counter, took the paper, and walked out.

Something wrong? Something wrong? Everything was wrong. Wrong. Wrong. Wrong. First Mulligan had to make a phone call. Then . . .

Bernard Browne lay in bed next to Louise Mundy. Her bed. Long slender fingers gently stroked the side of his face. "I appreciate your going through the motions, Brownie, but you were miles away."

"Guess so. I'm sorry . . ."

"Well, it wasn't *that* bad. Where were you, Toledo? 'Nam? Some case? Or Mulligan? It's his sister, right?"

"I'm the last one who talked to her—except for whoever killed her. Just before she hung up, she said there was a knock on the door. Damn it, Louise, I should've—"

"Should've what? What could you have done? You were hundreds of miles away."

"I don't know what I could've done, but I know what I'm going to do."

"What?"

"Go to Salt Lake City."

"Will the department let you?"

"I've got some time off coming."

"What are you going to do in Salt Lake City?"

"Number one, that's where the funeral will be ..."

"Brownie I know how you feel about Mulligan."

"Do you?"

"Enough to almost be jealous."

"What're you talking about?"

"If he and I were both drowning, I'm not so sure which one of us you'd save."

Browne brought her closer and kissed her. He smiled and touched her lips with his fingers.

"I'd save you both—or die trying."

"My hero. My lover ... My husband?"

"Louise ..."

"You're right. This is a not a good time to talk about it. But it's a good *place*." She smiled. "I'll take a rain check. Okay?"

"Okay."

"What's number two?"

"Huh?"

"What are you're going to do in Salt Lake City, besides go to the funeral?"

"It was the scene of the crime."

"Bernie you're a Las Vegas cop. I don't think the Salt Lake City Police Department will appreciate you playing buttinsky."

"I'm just a friend of the family, in fact I'm part of the family, the only family they've got."

"And Mulligan won't be there ..."

"You missed the point."

"What point?"

"I'm afraid he *will* be."

Chapter 15

The newspaper was on the seat next to Mulligan as he drove the Camaro toward Salt Lake City.

He remembered the illustrated brochure Annie had sent him after she and Tom were married and settled there. It was her subtle way of suggesting he leave Toledo and come somewhere west where there was better climate and better opportunity, somewhere like Salt Lake City maybe. The brochure was filled with pictures and information.

Salt Lake City was founded July, 24, 1847, by a group of Mormon pioneers. The Mormons are members of the Church of Jesus Christ of Latter-day Saints.

He remembered his first visit almost a year after they were married. Tom took him fishing, just the two of them. After about an hour Tom put down the rod and reel as the small boat bobbed gently at anchor in the lake. "Mulligan," he said, "I know how much you love your sister. So do I. I just want you to know I'll always love her. I'll always take care of her. That's one thing you'll never have to worry about." Tom picked up the rod and reel. "I just wanted you to know that. Now let's catch some fish."

Salt Lake County comprises an area of 746 square miles. The county is bordered on the west by the Great Salt Lake and on the east by the Wasatch Mountains. There are six major canyons which drain into the valley providing residents with water for drinking and for recreational pursuits.

He remembered stopping to visit Annie just before leaving for Vietnam. She was pregnant and more beautiful than she had ever been in her life. She hugged him and kissed him and he could feel her belly swollen with the life that stirred inside. "Mulligan, if you see Tom tell him I love him, tell him to take care of himself. And you take care of yourself. The two of you don't have to win the war all by yourselves."

Salt Lake City has served as the capital of the state since Utah was admitted to the Union on January 4, 1896. The city is most famous as the worldwide headquarters of the Mormon Church, and for Temple Square, the Mormon Tabernacle Choir, the Great Salt Lake, and world-class ski resorts.

He remembered coming back to Salt Lake City after Vietnam and staying with Annie for a month before going off to Langley to join the CIA, or at least take the tests, after being recruited by one of the Agency people in Saigon. The Agency man had liked what he saw in Mulligan the soldier. He gave him a number to call and suggested that, after his tour of duty, Mulligan the soldier ought to consider becoming Mulligan the spook.

Annie had already sold the house where she and Tom had lived, the one with the baby's room she had prepared, and had moved into a smaller house. A house without memories.

> Beehive State is Utah's nickname. Utahans relate the beehive symbol to industry and the pioneer virtues of thrift and perseverance. The state flower is the sego lily; the state tree is the blue spruce; and the state bird is the California gull; the time zone is Mountain.

He remembered coming back to Salt Lake City after his first overseas assignment for Keyes. Mulligan was sure he would be killed on his next assignment, or the one after that, or, if not then, sometime soon. Like Francis Macomber, his would be a short and happy life. Meantime he'd grab what he could. That's when he met Claire.

Gorgeous red-haired Claire. Persuasive, pervasive Claire. Maybe the marriage wouldn't be perfect. Maybe it wouldn't last. But what the hell was? What the hell did?

He would have to get permission from Keyes and Company to marry. Company policy and part of the deal he agreed to when he signed up. Claire promised to wait. Nothing better came along, so she waited—with a little fun and games in between, Mulligan later found out.

Salt Lake County's projected population was 690,000 in 1985. The 1990 projected population for Salt Lake City is 782,000.

After Mulligan almost got killed and received his first Distinguished Intelligence Medal, Keyes generously gave Mulligan permission to commit ceremonial suicide by permitting him to marry Claire. Mulligan and Claire drove to Las Vegas, went through the ceremony, and stayed for their honeymoon. Annie sent a two-word telegram. "Good Luck."

Salt Lake City's official elevation is 4,330.35 feet above sea level. However, the city is situated on land once covered by prehistoric Lake Bonneville. The old lake bed's elevation varies.

So did Mulligan's marriage.

The eastern and northern portions of the city are located on a series of lake terraces or former beaches which are known locally as 'benches.'

Mulligan decided to bench himself from the company game and come back to ever-loving Claire before she could collect on his life-insurance policy.

What kind of a job is a former soldier and spook suited for? He had saved nearly forty thousand dollars in spite of Claire. He was going to think it over for a long time. But Claire didn't like that. Mulligan's being around so much was interfering with her social life.

Salt Lake City's average daytime temperature for the warmest month, July, is 87.2 degrees Fahrenheit, and for the coldest month, January, is 37 degrees Fahrenheit. Summer nights are cool due to canyon breezes.

It was on a cool summer night; Claire had already met and melted Jason Lewis who came to town for a convention. Prior to that she had managed to spend twenty of Mulligan's forty thousand dollars. During the divorce proceedings she drew out the second twenty thousand, and on that cool summer night she skipped Salt Lake City— as the song goes—with Mulligan's hard-earned cash.

Snowfall averages 54.0 inches per year in the valley. The surrounding mountain resorts receive over 34 feet of snow. Measurable snow usually falls in the valley beginning in November and continues through April. Heaviest accumulation in the valley is in January when an average of 11.9 inches of snow is received. Temperatures generally vary enough during the winter months so that a buildup of ice and snow does not occur.

It was still summer, but inside Mulligan there was a buildup of ice—and blood—and guilt. In all his years as a spook he had been scrupulously careful not to involve Annie in the slightest way, in any assignment. He never told her when he would be going, or where, or when he would return.

In the course of those assignments he assumed various

identities, used different passports. Annie was privy to none of this. She knew there was someone named Keyes and someone else called Miss Fetzer, that was all she knew. It wasn't that Mulligan couldn't trust his sister, he would have trusted her more than he trusted Keyes, but the less she knew the safer she and Mulligan both were.

This time Mulligan had slipped up. They had traced her through his first phone call from the motel in Las Vegas. But at that time he could not have known that five million dollars would land in his lap. Even when he picked up that briefcase at Flo's after the bloodletting, he didn't know what was inside. It could have been dope or diamonds or the basis for blackmail. What he did know was that all those people died because of it. *He* could have been killed because of it, and he wasn't going to walk out of there leaving it behind. He wasn't going to stay and wait either, because at any minute some men with guns might appear and claim it—and Mulligan's life.

He never imagined that it would claim Annie's life. Calling her the second time was a risk, but it would have been a bigger risk not to call. He had to get her away, but he hadn't wanted to worry her—or have her worry about him—so he'd tried to play it as cool as he could and still get her out of harm's way. And now Annie was cold. Cold and dead. And this summer was the winter of Mulligan's discontent.

Damn the five million dollars, and damn Mulligan. But the ones who would really be damned were the ones who had killed Annie.

Mulligan knew he was driving and then walking into a trap, but he had been trapped before. So far he had walked out and the trappers hadn't. This time might be different.

But Mulligan didn't care. All he cared about was killing Annie's killers.

By sunset he had reached the Great Salt Lake. He drove east on Highway 80 past Salt Lake City International Airport and swung onto North Temple and across the Jordan River. He headed east past the majestic six-spired temple that dominated the lavish, moonlit grounds of the ten-acre site in the center of the city. He went through Main Street and turned south on State Street to Sunnyside Avenue where he turned left.

He drove, dreading the thought of his destination, until he saw the sign.

Then, somehow, that other set of reflexes took over, as it always had—on the football fields, on the battlefields, on the landing fields. In the back alleys and on the cutthroat corners of the world, that surge of readiness and confidence would well up whenever he knew his life was at stake.

Mulligan slowed down at the funeral home.

Chapter 16

The small parking lot next to the Croye Funeral Home was full. In fact there were cars parked on both sides of the street and some around the corner. But even if the lot had been empty, Mulligan would not have parked in it. There was only one driveway out of the lot.

He pulled the Camaro around the corner and found a spot. He got out of the car, closed the door, but left it unlocked. He walked across the grass and onto the pavement leading to the entrance.

The cars parked around the Croye Funeral Home were empty, all but one—the dark four-door Cadillac sedan. A rental.

There were five men inside. Crago was at the wheel, Zable on the passenger side, and three men were in the back seat. The Seymour brothers, Vic and Charlie. Emile DuMonte completed the quintet. All armed. All professionals.

"Bingo," Crago smiled.

"Not yet," said Zable. "It'll be bingo when he's sitting between us. Wait five minutes, then go get him."

"It's awfully crowded in there," Charlie observed. "They must be having a sale."

"Yeah," Vic said. "Why don't we wait till he comes out?"

"Because he may not come out this way," Zable explained just above a whisper. "There're other doors—and windows. This way you know exactly where he'll be. With his sister."

"Right," Crago added.

"Glad you agree."

"He can't be too bright," Vic noted, "walking in there like that."

"He's bright enough to have five million dollars," Zable said. "But not for long."

Mulligan opened the door and entered.

Hospitals and funeral parlors have something in common. Maybe it's because one is just a step removed from the other. And they both try to camouflage their contents with odors. The hospitals employ antiseptics, disinfectants, and germicides to dispel the smells bred by sickness. Funeral parlors resort to flowers, air fresheners, and even organ music to dismiss the odor of death.

On the hospital operating table you've got a chance, usually a better than even chance, of surviving and walking away from the odor of the anesthetic.

Inside the box in a funeral parlor, it can only get worse.

Mulligan stepped into the entry hall that centered several "slumber rooms" of varying sizes and pastel colors.

To the left of Mulligan organ music and singing emanated from the largest, double-doored room. One of the doors was slightly ajar, and it was evident that the chamber had been filled to capacity. A sign in flowing script designated it as the Kingdom Come Hall.

To Mulligan's right the Elysium Room, smaller and with a single door, was also occupied, almost to capacity. The door was open. Nobody sang, but deep sighs and soft moans escaped into the center hall.

A man appeared through a door marked OFFICE and approached Mulligan. He was no less than thirty-eight and no more than forty, no shorter than five-eight, no taller than five-ten. He wore a conservative blue suit, with a carnation in the buttonhole.

"May I help you, sir?" I am Edward Croye, Jr." He spoke in soft sympathetic tones. Mulligan recognized the voice.

"Ann Robbins," he said.

"Yes, of course. May I inquire, are you related to the deceased?"

"I'm the one who made the call and wired the money."

"Of course. We selected the casket you described, and placed the picture inside as you requested."

"Okay." There was a touch of impatience in Mulligan's voice.

"She's in the Sunset Room." Edward Croye, Jr., ushered Mulligan toward a small room at the far end of the hall. "There's someone with her now."

Mulligan paused. "What's he look like?"

Croye *fils* took a step closer to the Sunset Room and pointed with a soft, graceful hand toward the open door. "It's a lady."

Mulligan could see the figure of a woman sitting on a folding chair not far from the casket, but her back was to the door. He could also see that the casket was open.

"I wanted the casket closed."

"I'm sorry, sir, you didn't specify."

Mulligan hadn't specified. His mind was cluttered with other things when he made the call.

"I guess I didn't."

"We worked very hard to ... Well, she does look beautiful."

"Okay." This time Mulligan's tone spelled dismissal.

"I hope that everything is satisfactory," Croye said with practiced earnestness, and walked toward the office.

How the hell could it be satisfactory, Mulligan thought, I'm going in to see my dead sister.

But he went in.

There were six rows of folding chairs flanking both sides of the aisle. The woman sat in the second row to Mulligan's right as he approached the casket. Her head was slightly bowed. She made no acknowledgment of his presence, nor did Mulligan look at her as he walked by, but he made sure she remained within sight, in case she made any move.

He stopped just a step away from his dead sister. Annie did look beautiful. Mulligan was sorry that he had taken that tone with Croye. It couldn't have been easy to conceal the effects of the beating. It took more make-up than Annie ever wore, but that wasn't their fault. It couldn't be helped. And they had placed a soft, blue silk scarf about her throat to cover those marks. The blue scarf matched Annie's eyes, the eyes that Mulligan never would see again.

And as Mulligan had requested, they had placed the

"smiling" picture of Annie and Tom inside the casket. I hope you two are dancing somewhere together, Mulligan thought. He could hear Tom's voice singing the words to "Dancing In The Dark," *Time hurries by; we're here, then gone.*

Time did hurry by, too fast—for both of them. Tom paid the price of going to war. But Annie, that was different.

"Sé 'agapo, my sweet sister," Mulligan said to himself, and added, "I'll get the sons of bitches."

Peripherally, Mulligan could see the woman rise. She paused a moment, then walked toward him. She was attractive, and could have been even more so, but her hairdo and attire at this time did not conspire to accent her physical appearance.

As she came closer and Mulligan took note of her, he was somehow reminded of Frances Fetzer—the same heart-shaped face, hair a lighter copper, younger, taller and more svelte, at least from what he could tell through the apparel she wore. But her face was sadder than Miss Fetzer's had ever been. Her eyes, the color of the distant sunlit sea, were now moist.

"You'd be Ann's brother." She said.

Mulligan said nothing.

"I'm Abbey Bain." She looked at Annie. "We took a poetry class together at night."

Abbey Bain extended her hand to Mulligan. "I'm so sorry."

Mulligan took her hand briefly and nodded an acknowledgment.

"We'd go out for coffee after class and she ... well I think I could have picked you out of any crowd ... she talked... Oh, excuse me, I'm sure you'd like to have some time with her."

Mulligan still did not speak.

Abbey Bain understood. She started to walk away but added, "I just came back into town and heard what happened... I had to come by."

"Thank you," Mulligan said softly.

"Good night." She walked toward the door.

Mulligan took a step to the casket and lowered the lid.

As Abbey Bain approached the door, three men entered. They made way as she passed by them and left the room.

Then they closed ranks. Crago, Vic, and Charlie walked down the aisle, Crago a step in front with Vic and Charlie on either side. The brothers' coats were unbuttoned, their right hands near their belts.

Mulligan turned and faced them. His expression held no surprise, fear, or emotion. It was impossible to tell what he was thinking. He was thinking, God I hope you're the ones who did it. Then it would be over right here and now, with Annie in the room. I hope to Christ you're the ones. I hope you're not just stooges. Please be the killers.

Crago stopped four feet away. A smart distance. Not close enough to be hit or grabbed, but close enough to draw and fire point-blank.

"You're coming with us."

"Who're you?"

"Maybe we're cops."

"Maybe you're not."

"Either way," Crago shrugged, "you're coming."

"All right."

"That's smart." Crago smiled. "But you were dumb enough to show up in the first place."

"Yeah." Mulligan nodded toward the casket. "You have anything to do with that?"

"Just an assist. You'll meet the scorer."

"What's his name?"

"Why not?" Crago shrugged again. "You'll find out anyhow. The name is Zable. You've got something he wants. Move!"

Mulligan paused for only an instant. Damn! It wasn't these three. They were stooges. That figured. They might have been pros, but they weren't elite. When they first came in and confronted him, they should have been farther apart and on each side of Mulligan instead of all bunched up. They had stood in each other's line of fire. Not for long but for too long. Had Mulligan made his move then, one of them probably would have shot another. But at that time Mulligan didn't want to make a move, not until he found out what he needed to know.

By now they had fanned out and were in better positions. Still, he couldn't let them take him to the killer. Zable might be miles away, and if Mulligan went along, when they got there Zable would call the shots, have all the advantages. No, it would have to be another time, another place—when and where some of the advantages would be Mulligan's. At least he'd found out what he needed to know. He'd found out about Zable.

For the time being all Mulligan had to do was figure a way to get out of the funeral parlor alive. They hadn't even frisked him yet. A man and woman stood just outside the open door, talking and occasionally glancing into the Sunset Room, so, given the circumstances, the delivery boys were being as circumspect as three gunsels could be.

But Mulligan knew damn well that once they got him

outside the building they'd search him. They'd probably do more than that. A rap behind the ear with a sap, or the barrel of a gun, might be in order.

Mulligan would have to make his break on the inside. He hoped that the three stooges would slip up again, even for just a moment, as they had when first entering the Sunset Room.

But if they didn't, Mulligan would have to manufacture a slipup.

"I said move!" Crago repeated.

Mulligan moved, with Vic and Charlie on either side and Crago now behind him.

As they went through the door of the Sunset Room, Mulligan spotted a fourth torpedo idling in the center hall, just inside the entrance. He wasn't tough to spot because Vic and Charlie nodded to him and he nodded back. They definitely were not elite. Mulligan wouldn't've been surprised if they had exchanged winks. Still, the idler at the entrance lengthened the odds against Mulligan just that much more.

The organ music from Kingdom Come Hall now swelled to the accompaniment of nearly a hundred voices chorusing "Nearer My God to Thee." The singing was led by Reverend Mason Douglas, a rope-thin man in his mid seventies. He wore pince-nez glasses and had a curiously deep voice for someone his size. It was as if his voice were being dubbed by some basso profundo. The object of the serenade lay in a coffin at the front of the room. The man who reposed within looked like an older facsimile of the reverend. The resemblance was logical since the deceased indeed was Madison Douglas, Mason's father, who had made it into his mid nineties.

When it appeared that Zable's foursome would succeed in escorting the object of their assignment out of the hallway and into the night, the door of the Elysium Room swung fully open and a platoon of mourners, now led by Edward Croye, Jr., dispersed from within. Some made their way to the front door; others stayed and mingled, discussing the departed one, who of course remained, for the time being, inside the Elysium Room.

Ever mindful of the value of a satisfied customer, Mr. Croye wasted no time. When he saw Mulligan, he headed directly for him, excusing himself as he brushed past Charlie Seymour, whose hand was inside his coat.

"Sir," Croye intoned. "Is everything satisfactory, sir?"

"Everything is fine," Crago immediately volunteered.

But Mulligan stopped, as even more mourners streamed out of the Elysium Room and crowded into the hallway.

"Just one thing, Edward." Mulligan's voice was warm and friendly. "One little thing . . ."

"Yes?" Edward took a step closer, and as he did Mulligan grabbed his left lapel, crushing his carnation, and rammed him hard into Crago who had stepped forward.

Vic and Charlie both went for their guns, but suddenly there was a gun in Mulligan's hand. He fired first, hitting Charlie directly above his left eye.

People screamed and scattered. Some fell to the carpet, some fought each other to get back into the Elysium Room and close the door. Two ladies fainted, others made for the entrance where Emile stood, gun unholstered now, trying to aim at Mulligan.

Vic remained momentarily paralyzed at seeing his brother killed. Mulligan had already kicked Crago in the groin sending him to his knees.

Mulligan whirled and slammed through the double doors and into Kingdom Come Hall.

He raced up the aisle, past the startled congregation; stopped near the Reverend Douglas at the side of the reverend's father's coffin and fired into the ceiling.

"Jesus Christ!" exclaimed the reverend.

Pandemonium ensued. The gathering, composed mostly of senior citizens, rose as fast as they could, toppling chairs, knocking into each other, invoking the Lord's name for help, and generally stampeding to get out through the doors.

Vic and Crago, who held a gun in one hand and his crotch with the other, were knocking people out of the way and down, fighting to get through the scrambling seniors and closer to Mulligan.

Crago shoved Reverend Douglas out of the way and hollered above the din to Vic. "Zable wants him alive."

"Fuck Zable," Vic hollered back. "He killed Charlie!"

Mulligan looked for a window to jump through, but there was none. In the early confusion, Reverend Douglas and others had bumped hard against the old man's coffin, knocking it off its stand, tumbling the deceased out of his container and onto the floor.

While there was no window, Mulligan spotted a door on one side of Kingdom Come Hall. He stepped over the body of Madison Douglas; who had not been outfitted with shoes, ran to the door, opened it, went through, and slammed it shut. He had entered another "slumber room," the smallest of them all. It was vacant and had no window, just an open door leading back to the hallway and the outpouring mourners from Kingdom Come Hall.

There just wasn't any other place for Mulligan to go.

As he headed out of the room toward the hallway, Crago and Vic opened the adjoining door from Kingdom Come Hall, but Mulligan temporarily discouraged their pursuit by firing two shots in their direction. Crago and Vic ducked back long enough for Mulligan to run into the hallway; where Emile stood by the entrance warding off the herd of shrieking departees as they poured through the exit. Charlie Seymour still lay on the floor. He was still dead.

Mulligan caught sight of a door marked PRIVATE, so naturally he opened it and went in. It led to a small landing and a dimly lit stairway to the basement. Mulligan slapped the door shut and looked for a lock. There was none. He raced down the stairs to the floor below and stopped in front of a closed door. The sign on it read PREPARATION ROOM. There was an elevator to his left which obviously led back up to the hallway, so that was out. Besides, an elevator was a no-good place to get into when you're being chased.

Mulligan quickly tried the Preparation Room door. Unlocked. If it hadn't been, he would have broken in. Mulligan opened the door.

Darkness. His hand crawled along the inside of the doorway wall until he felt a switch. He flicked it and the lights went on, illuminating the interior of the Preparation Room—preparation, a euphemism for embalming.

The preparation table in the center of the room was empty, but nearby on tables and shelves were surgical instruments, hoses, jars, bottles, and assorted sundries. Also within the room were three gurneys sustaining three cadavers covered by rubber sheets from their respective necks down. Two female cadavers, one male.

Mulligan closed the door and hastily surveyed the rest of the territory. To his good fortune, there was a medium-size window high on the opposite wall that connected to the exterior grounds.

Mulligan pushed the gurney with the man's body against the window wall, then he had a promising thought as his eyes fell on several bottles on a shelf, bottles with prominent labels.

He knew that upstairs his pursuers would see the door marked PRIVATE at any second, if they hadn't already, and they would continue their pursuit—at least one or two of them would—down the stairs and into the Preparation Room. Let them come. The more the better. Mulligan moved toward the bottles.

Emile had seen Mulligan disappear through the PRIVATE door. By the time he got there he was joined by Crago and Vic.

When they opened the door and saw the stairway, Crago motioned to the other two. "You guys go down there. I'll stay and cover the upstairs; my balls are killing me."

Vic and Emile made their way down the dark stairs, guns at the ready. Vic noticed the sliver of light at the bottom of the Preparation Room door and pointed to it. Emile nodded as they continued their descent.

By then Mulligan had locked the brake on the gurney, jumped aboard—straddling the cadaver—and unlocked the window. He now faced the door, gun in hand.

Outside, the two men reached the doorway, looked at each other for a moment and nodded. Vic's hand moved toward the knob.

The door burst open. Vic and Emile charged through with guns drawn. On the inner threshold of the door there now was a large pool of liquid with three bottles lying empty and one bottle standing full.

The bottles were labeled Embalmers Cleaning Fluid—Flammable.

For an instant Vic and Emile fought for footing on the wet, slippery floor. In that instant Mulligan, atop the gurney, fired and hit the full bottle. It exploded. Blue and yellow flames spread across the pool and upward onto Vic's and Emile's legs. Instinctively both men dropped their guns and reached down to beat at their blazing pant legs. But by then four-foot flames leaped from the pool and turned the two of them into human torches, screaming in agony.

Mulligan watched from the gurney until both men were immolated and could scream no more.

The rest of the room caught fire. The three cadavers along with Vic and Charlie would not be buried. They'd be cremated.

Mulligan tucked the Beretta into his belt, boosted up from the gurney to the window, and hoisted himself through, feeling the heat of the flames consuming the room behind him.

The heat felt good.

The outside of the Croye Funeral Home had turned into a three-ring circus without clowns.

But there were over a hundred frightened men and women scrambling, babbling, pointing, hollering, and screaming "Call the police!" Some were trying to find who ever it was they came in with. Some were making for their cars in the parking lot and on the street. Cars that were driving by slowed down and stopped to observe the confusion.

Zable still sat in the Cadillac. Now the window was rolled down, and there was a gun in his lap.

Crago came out of the entrance, made his way through the crowd, and reached the Cadillac.

"Did he come out?"

"Would I be sitting here if he did?" Zable replied. "Where's the rest of 'em?"

"I guess they're still inside. They went after him—down in the basement. We'll get him!"

"Sure you will."

Crago turned and started to leave.

"Wait a minute," Zable snapped. "Where you going?"

"Back inside."

"You stay here. Right here!"

A blue-haired woman pointed toward the funeral home and cried, "Fire!"

Others in the crowd took up the cry as flames shot up and out of the basement window.

Edward Croye, Jr., stood mumchance, watching the latest dreadful development.

Mulligan made his way across the lawn toward the side street. His car was blocked by traffic.

A car bolted past the others and screeched to a skidding halt. Mulligan pulled the gun from his belt, ready to aim, but the passenger door flew open and a woman's voice ordered, "Get in!"

Crago spotted Mulligan and hollered, "There he is!" He fired in spite of the crowd and missed. Mulligan fired back shattering part of the Cadillac's windshield.

Mulligan jumped into the front seat, and Abbey Bain burned rubber even before he could close the door.

With this latest development, people dove for safety

onto the grass and sidewalk. Some fled across the street, barely avoiding traffic.

Come on, let's go!" Zable commanded, and Crago ran to the driver's side of the Cadillac.

Edward Croye, Jr., still stood paralyzed on the same spot.

The Cadillac swung out from the curb, scraping against a moving car. Horns blared, people cursed, and somewhere in the distance a siren screamed.

"Fucking windshield," Crago cursed. "I can hardly see through it."

"They're turning left."

"I got 'em."

But Crago didn't have them. There were several vehicles in between. Crago's palm shoved against the horn, then he pulled out of his lane, crossed the line to the left into the oncoming traffic, slicing between a taxi cab and a bus, just missing a pedestrian who was crossing with the light.

Abbey Bain drove a black Honda Prelude and the way she drove it her name could have been Andretti. Mulligan glanced at her patrician profile, not quite as patrician as Miss Fetzer's but still in the classic mold. He could barely believe that this was the same sad lady he had met in the Sunset Room.

Those eyes that had been lachrymose now glistened with energy. The hands that had trembled slightly were strong and firm on the wheel, but not tense. There was a faint trace of a smile, a challenging catch-me-if-you-can, confident smile, on what Mulligan noticed were remarkably expressive lips.

How do you do, Miss Abbey Bain? he said to himself. You do damn well, he answered.

Abbey Bain tore through the street, passing every moving thing from both the left and the right. She had turned left on 1300 East with the Cadillac doing its best to keep within sight. She then passed a station wagon from the left, turned sharply in front of it just before a corner, and swerved right onto 2100 South as the station wagon braked to a swerving stop.

Crago hit his brakes and barely managed the right turn after landing on the wrong lane in the turning.

"Who's driving that goddamn thing?" said Zable.

"Fucked if I know." Crago maneuvered the Cad back onto the proper lane.

Abbey looked back and saw that they were still in view.

"Let there be darkness," she said. Her hand hit the panel and all the lights—headlights, taillights, and panel lights—went off. Her foot pressed harder on the accelerator. She ignored a stop sign and sped right across the intersection.

Mulligan cleared his throat. He peered through the windshield toward the dark street in front of them.

"Is your insurance paid up?" he inquired.

"Car . . . or life?"

"Both."

She smiled, honked, and weaved in and out of traffic.

A Salt Lake City Police car cruised from the opposite direction. The officers within could not fail to notice that the Honda Prelude was violating a number of traffic laws. The police car, siren and klaxon blaring, negotiated an abrupt U-turn and fell in several yards behind the Cadillac which was also disregarding the posted speed limit.

"There's a cop car behind us." Crago pointed with his thumb toward the rear window. "What do we do?"

"Keep going."

"Okay." Crago squinted through the cracked windshield. "Where'd they go!"

They had gone right through a red light at no less than seventy-five miles per hour.

Zable caught sight of the disappearing car and pointed ahead. "There!"

Crago hit the accelerator, zooming through the intersection, but he didn't make it.

A Dodge Van had the right of passage and was halfway through the crossing when broadsided by the Cadillac. The impact hurled both Zable and Crago into the windshield. Crago hit head-on. Zable managed to twist so his shoulder and back took most of the damage.

The policeman driving the pursuing car slammed on the brake and spun the wheel, but could not harness the car completely. It skidded sideways and crunched into the trunk of the Cadillac. At the same time, a convertible with the right of way, moving south on State Street, barreled into the passenger side of the Cadillac, hurling Zable against Crago.

In spite of the collision, the police car's siren and klaxon still screamed and flashed.

Mulligan looked back at the pileup. "By George, I think you've done it!"

Abbey winked.

Mulligan pointed to the panel. "I also think it's okay to use the lights again."

"You're the captain." She pulled the knob.

"Say, where'd you learn to drive like that?"

"From my mother."

"Right. Did your mother ever take a drink?"

"Yep."

"Could *you* use a drink?"

"Yep ... a double."

"Let's find a club."

"I've got a better idea."

"What's that?"

"There's a jug of gin in the trunk. Let's find a spot where there aren't a lot of people around."

"That *is* a better idea. Much better."

"We'll stop and get some ice."

Chapter 17

The Great Salt Lake is, with the exception of the Dead Sea, the saltiest body of water in the world. Its salinity varies from 5 to 15%, making it nearly twice as salty as any ocean. Streams that originate in the Wasatch Mountains and other nearby mountain ranges flow into the Great Salt Lake, carrying large amounts of dissolved minerals. As the lake has no outlet, all of these minerals are trapped in it. The continual process of evaporation reduces the amount of water, thereby increasing its salinity.

The Great Salt Lake is a remnant of prehistoric Lake Bonneville which once covered 20,000 square miles of land in Utah, Nevada, and Idaho. The lake is presently 92 miles long and 48 miles wide.

The blanket where Mulligan and Abbey Bain sat took up only a tiny portion of that lake's shoreline.

Moonlight splayed against the water and beach. They had found this isolated area only a few minutes ago. It was as if they were visiting another planet, just the two of them, traveling to a different world.

Within the last hour there had been confrontation, gunshots, death, fire, more gunshots, panic, and a car chase ending in collision. A collision that did not involve Mulligan, thanks to a beautiful lady who, until that evening, he didn't even know existed.

It was fortunate for Mulligan that she did. He had enough confidence in himself to believe that he would have escaped even if she hadn't come along, but he was glad that she had. However, by helping him she had put herself in jeopardy. The gunsel and whoever was with him probably hadn't gotten close enough to be able to identify her, but maybe they had been close enough to catch her license plate before she turned off the lights. With all the confusion, traffic, and speed, the odds were against it, but not one hundred percent.

Abbey didn't seem concerned. She looked out at the lake and sipped from the plastic glass containing ice and gin from the quart of Gordon's resting on the blanket between them. Her hair had fallen loose, she had taken off her shoes and had undone the top two buttons of her Katharine Hepburn blouse, and as in the lyrics to the song Bing Crosby used to sing, moonlight became her, it went with her hair.

"Well," said Mulligan, taking a drink of gin from his plastic cup, "here's to our first anniversary."

"How's that?"

"We've known each other for about an hour. It's been swell."

"I think so. But it seems like I've known you for a long time."

"Why? Because of Annie?"

"Yes ... Does it hurt you to talk about her?"

"No." But Mulligan changed the subject. "Do you always travel with booze and blanket, and derring-do?"

"No, but as I said, I just got into town. My bags are still in the trunk."

"I noticed."

"Haven't even checked into a hotel yet."

"That's a coincidence. Neither have I. Don't you live in Salt Lake City?"

"Not anymore. Just passing through."

"West?"

"West. How about you? What are your plans?"

"That depends." Mulligan took another drink and changed the subject again. "It figures ..."

"What does?"

"That you'd be a gin man, sister."

"I can take it or leave it."

"I'm glad you took it tonight. The rest of it doesn't figure."

"The rest of what?"

"Why risk your skin to save somebody you don't even know? Why?"

"Two reasons. One, I liked Ann and what she said about you. Even though she didn't tell me what you really do, since the army, still she said a lot about you ... when you were kids ..."

Mulligan shook his head.

"What's the matter?" she asked.

"The second reason better be a doozy."

"It is." She was silent for a moment.

"Go ahead."

"I don't have a whole hell of a lot to lose, Mulligan."

Mulligan looked her up and down, and smiled. "From where I sit, you do."

"You know what they say about appearances." She raised her glass and motioned toward the quart of Gordon's. "Can I have another hit?"

"It's your bottle." Mulligan poured the gin into her glass, then put some into his own. "And your story. Go on."

"Ever hear of multiple myeloma?"

"No."

"Neither had I until about nine months ago. I remember it was on a Thursday. What day were you born, Mulligan?"

"Tuesday."

"Tuesday's child is full of grace. Anyhow I had a date to go skiing over the long weekend starting that Friday. Then I found out from the doctor that I had another date. In a year, two at the most. It's a bone affliction—plain talk, a *disease*—moves slowly; no pain until the last couple of months. Then there *is* pain, plenty of it, and it moves fast. Far as I'm concerned, the faster the better."

"Isn't there anything—"

"Mulligan, I just came back from Johns Hopkins. I took my 'final examination'—and flunked it."

"Another opinion?"

"I've had them. This was the court of last resort. It's okay. As they say, I've put my affairs in order. I talked about it with Ann. She used to console me, and now she ... Well, let's just say that at least I've had time to get ready."

"Nobody's ever ready."

"I guess you're right. Still, as the man wrote, 'It's a necessary end, and it will come when it will come.' Those people at the mortuary tried to hasten your end tonight."

"Not quite true."

"No?"

"They're not going to kill me."

"Do *they* know that?"

"At least, not yet."

"Why? Do they have a certain date in mind?"

"No, but I've got something they want. 'Til they get it, they won't kill me. They can't."

"I hope you've got it ditched some place deep."

"That I do."

"*Bueno.*"

"Miss Bain, you know what?"

"What?"

"I'm glad you came along."

"So am I."

"Don't you want to know what it is?"

"What what is?"

"What they want."

She finished her drink. Then Abbey Bain stood framed against the moonlight, with the Great Salt Lake behind her. She unbuttoned the other four buttons on her Katharine Hepburn blouse, slipped it behind her shoulders, and let it drop onto the blanket. On the left side of her hip, she zipped down the summer skirt. It, too, fell to the blanket. She reached behind her, unsnapping the gossamer-lace brassiere; worked the straps over her shoulders and let it fall to her bare feet. Her thumbs hooked onto her bikini panties, stretched them free from the curves of her hips, so they, too, dropped to the blanket, encircling her feet. She stepped free and, naked, stood before him. In the distant sky a star fell, but Mulligan barely noticed.

If there was a more inviting body, Mulligan had never seen it.

"Mulligan, I know what *I* want." She turned and walked across the sand toward the water.

Mulligan set the plastic glass down on the blanket. Abbey reached the water's edge and seemed to glide into the Great Salt Lake as it covered her ankles, calves, and thighs. Then she paused, turned, and faced the beach and Mulligan.

Her long and slender arms extended below the hourglass of her white waist and hips, her fingers barely touching the water. The moon, high to her left, emphasized her breasts while casting twin, circled shadows beneath.

Mulligan rose and undressed. She waited without moving until he walked from the beach into the water and very close to her. His hands, too, were at his sides even as his lips gently touched hers.

He scooped a palmful of water with his hand and let it drip onto her left shoulder near her throat. The droplets trickled onto her breast and downward, following the inner curve, to the flat of her midsection and disappeared below. She put her arms behind him and drew him against her. One of his hands went to the back of her neck, the other around her waist. Her body was firm but pliant, her lips tender and knowing. Neither of them hurried the moment. They took their time, their bodies pressing hard against each other, then relaxing, adjusting slightly and pressing again.

"Mulligan," she said, "you've got a good body."

"And vice versa."

"But sometime I'd like to hear how you got all those scars."

"Okay, I'll tell you . . . sometime."

She scooped up a palmful of water and let it drip onto his throat and down his chest, "It really is salty, isn't it?"

"Is it?"

"Let's find out." She surface-dove into the water and swam away.

He followed, caught up in a few strokes, and took her in his arms. The water did not quite cover her breasts.

"You know," she said, "we can't sink in this lake."

"We can try."

He kissed her and pulled her down with him beneath the surface, still kissing her and tasting the salt. They stayed under for almost a minute pressed together, resisting the buoyancy of the lake and the need for each other.

They surfaced still locked together.

"Captain Mulligan, First Mate Abigail Bain requests permission to go ashore."

"For what purpose?"

"For the purpose of making love on a blanket."

"That's a good purpose. Permission granted."

They walked, holding hands, out of the lake and across the sand and onto the blanket.

He had not enjoyed sex since Claire left him, and for the year before that, sex with Claire had not been very enjoyable. It had just been a necessary release.

Abigail Bain changed all of that. She wrapped herself around him like no other woman ever had, her body warm and wet and wanting, her lips salty-sweet and tender.

Together they were silk and steel.

"Make love to me, Mulligan. Make love like it's our last night on earth."

Mulligan did. For all he knew it might be.

Chapter 18

A little more than two hours later, night had hit bottom. It wasn't going to get any darker.

Mulligan drove the Prelude northwest. Abbey's left hand cupped his right, which was palmed around the gear shift. Neither had spoken since they had left the lake ten minutes ago.

"You want to tell me where we're going?" she finally said.

"What makes you think we're both going to the same place?"

"The last couple of hours ... and other things. What if they *did* spot the license plates?"

"I don't think so. Too much happened too fast, but even if they did, they're not going to share it with the cops ... and speaking of cops, no matter how much juice those two buttons have got, they're going to have some explaining to do to the local fuzz. *And* they're going to have to get patched up. So now's the best time for us to move."

"Let me ask you again, you mind telling me where we're going?"

"I've got a secret little place."

"Ahh, Shangri-la, where we'll never grow old."

"Not exactly Shangri-la." Mulligan smiled. "But do you remember a place from the same movie called Karakal?"

"Karakal? . . . No."

"Well, when Ronald Colman was trying to find his way back to Shangri-la, he finally spotted a familiar pass and said 'This, I think, is Karakal . . . and beyond is Shangri-la and the Valley of the Blue Moon.' We're headed for Karakal."

"Does it have anything like a bed or shower?"

"Both."

"Ahh, Captain Mulligan. The great provider."

Mulligan pulled off the secondary road onto a dirt path. While covering the next two miles, he stopped twice to unhitch gates, pass through, then rehitch the latches. Soon they were driving parallel to the sound, then the sight of a free-flowing river with moon-washed rocks and boulders cleaving the churning white waters.

A hundred yards from the river there was a cabin, a hunting lodge. A jeep covered by a tarp was parked under the double porte-cochere. Mulligan pulled the Prelude in next to the jeep.

Abbey looked through the darkness toward the structure. "There's no welcome light on."

"Ain't that the truth. We got to write Tom Bodett a letter of complaint." They both exited the Honda. "Give me a hand with that tarp."

"What're you gonna do?"

"Cover your car till we can steal some plates." He pointed to the trunk. "How much of that stuff do you want to take inside?"

"Just the blue overnight bag ... and you."

Mulligan unlocked the trunk and took out the blue bag. Then they covered the Prelude with the tarp.

The key to the cabin was hidden under a rain barrel.

Mulligan unlocked the door, still holding onto the overnight bag, then turned to her.

"Mulligan," she smiled, "we can skip the threshold bit and just get on with the honeymoon."

She walked through the doorway; he followed, kicked the door shut, dropped the bag, put both arms around her, and kissed her.

They both were ready to get on with the honeymoon.

She started to undress and murmured, "So this is Karakal."

Most of these proceedings were observed in silence from a distance. The observer was a hooty owl clinging to a tree. But the hooty owl didn't give a hoot. After a while he turned his one open eye in the direction of the river and thought about who knows what.

Chapter 19

The next morning at seven fifteen Louise Mundy was driving Lieutenant Bernard Browne to McCarran in her Jaguar XJS-V12 convertible.

"No, Louise. *N-O*. Forget it!"

"Listen, Brownie, do you know how many favors I've done for that airline?"

"That's not the point, your Ladyship. The point is, I don't want you doing me any favors. I paid for a tourist ticket and I'm going to fly in the tourist section."

"It's all been taken care of; they had four empty first-class seats, and you've already been bumped up into one of them. Besides, you're getting too fat to fit into a tourist seat—especially with that rod. I'm talking about the one you take off in bed."

Browne had called ahead, and they were met by Marvin Hascal of McCarran Security, who took them around the metal detectors and straight to the gate. The passengers were already aboard.

"When you get on, have Miss Morrisson—she's the chief flight attendant—take you to the cabin and introduce you to Captain Roman. He knows you're carrying," Hascal said. "Happy landing, Lieutenant. Good-bye, Miss Mundy."

Browne dropped his carry-on bag and put his arms around Louise. "I'll see you in a couple of days."

"Wanna bet? 'Specially if you catch up with Mulligan. Just stay away from those Salt Lake City petooties, you're my man, see!"

"I thought you said I was getting fat..."

"I'll put you through some exercises when you get back. Now get out of here before I say something stupid."

Browne kissed her, then picked up his carry-on bag and headed onto the ramp as the flight to Salt Lake City was called for the last time.

Miss Morrisson, a petite, freckle-splattered, carrot-top greeted Browne, then knocked on the cabin door. When it was opened by the flight engineer, she ushered Browne inside.

"Captain Roman, this is Lieutenant Browne. Las Vegas Police."

Roman, a handsome gray-haired pelican, nodded unenthusiastically. "I understand you're carrying."

"That's right." Browne unbuttoned his jacket.

"Anything to do with any passengers aboard this flight?"

"No, Captain." Browne buttoned up.

"Then I wish you people would pack those things in suitcases so some nut can't take them away from you and shoot this plane full of holes. Ever try flying in a plane full of holes, Lieutenant?"

"Me, I pretend like this is a bus. And if it's any consolation, Captain Roman, nobody's taken this guy away in almost twenty years."

"Okay." There was a tone of annoyed dismissal in Roman's voice as he turned to the copilot. "Stan, let's go through the check list."

Miss Morrisson escorted Browne from the cabin to the first-class section where there were twelve seats. Four seats were empty. The other eight were occupied by Johnny Rice, Louis Lepitino, and six persuasive-looking men of assorted sizes and complexions. Their tickets were booked under the names of Allen, Blake, Cotter, Detroit, Escobar and Fanelli. But, between the bunch of them, over the years they had used enough names to fill the Sandusky Ohio telephone directory.

Upon spotting Browne, Lepitino in his subtle Italian style, nudged Rice, who already was looking at the detective through expensive prescription sunglasses.

As Miss Morrisson and Browne walked by, toward the vacant seats at the rear of First Class, Rice smiled. Browne didn't.

"This is your seat, Mr. Browne. May I bring you a drink? We're just about to take off."

"No, thanks, I'm fine." Browne sat next to the window and strapped himself into the seat belt.

Miss Morrisson and the other flight attendant went through the usual procedure of pointing out emergency exits, oxygen masks, and flotation pillows; and as usual, nobody paid the slightest heed.

The takeoff was smooth and soon a second round of drinks was being served in First Class. Browne ordered a large orange juice and was taking his second swallow when Johnny Rice rose with his Bloody Mary, walked back to Browne, and pointed to the empty seat next to the detective.

"Do you mind, Lieutenant?"

Browne didn't say yes and he didn't say no.

Rice sat. "Say, this is a coincidence!"

"I don't think so."

"Going to Salt Lake on a case?"

"Funeral."

"Oh."

"Maybe funerals."

"Yeah, I heard about Mulligan's sister . . ."

"I'll bet you did."

"What does that mean?"

"Whatever you want it to mean."

"Let's just be . . . ," Rice shrugged, "friends, like in the good ol' days."

"Okay, friend, why're *you* going to Salt Lake?"

"A little business."

"You need the dirty half-dozen," Browne waved at Rice's entourage, "to carry your luggage?"

"Just giving the boys a little change of venue."

"I hear Mulligan changed the venue of about half the Saint Louis contingent."

"Tell me, Lieutenant, do you think Mulligan is still in Salt Lake City?"

"I don't know." Browne shrugged. "But I'll tell you

one thing, bub, I wouldn't want to stand in the shoes of whoever killed his sister—no matter where he goes."

"Just for the record, Lieutenant, I never had anything to do with killing anybody—ever. Now, let's enjoy our breakfast."

"Right. Oh, Miss Morrisson." The smiling flight attendant was serving breakfast to the first-class passengers.

"Yes, Mr. Browne. What can I do for you?"

"Are there any empty seats back in the tourist section?"

"Well, yes ... but ..."

Browne unhitched his seat belt, rose, and walked in front of Rice and past the surprised flight attendant who was not nearly as surprised as Johnny Rice.

"Thank you, Miss Morrisson." Browne said. Then he disappeared through the curtain that divided First Class from Tourist.

The last time Rice had talked to Keelo, only a few hours ago, Keelo was as angry as Rice could ever remember. Angrier.

Keelo was an insomniac. Three hours of sleep was a marathon for him. Last night must have been a hundred-yard dash. Keelo was mad at his bed partner, mad because of the double-triple cross from Vegas to Chicago, mad because Mulligan got away with the five million, and madder yet because of what happened in Salt Lake City. Zable, whom Keelo considered the best, had set up Mulligan, but instead Mulligan turned the tables—shot one and waxed two of Zable's gorillas—and got away free as a bee, with Keelo's five million stashed in some honeycomb.

Besides that, Keelo didn't have any appreciable juice with the Salt Lake City Police Department and couldn't expect the cooperation he could get in other places.

Phil Keelo wasn't getting any stronger or any younger. More and more he had to prove himself—to the dames who got him through the night, to the people on the inside who worked for him and cast envious eyes on his empire, and to the people on the outside—hungry Young Turks who would risk life, limb, and the pursuit of the mundane in order to knock off number one. That was what Keelo had been for a long time, number one—in the history of this business an extraordinarily long time. So most of every night and every day, Phil Keelo had to prove himself—to himself.

When he had spoken to Rice just a few hours ago Keelo's instructions were, "You and Lepitino, and those six dwarfs you're so in love with, get on a morning flight to Salt Lake. Hook up with Zable at his hotel, and whatever's left of his gashouse gang, and call me. It's getting so I wouldn't trust the whole bunch of you with a box of Snickers Bars."

Before Rice could contribute to the conversation, Keelo had hung up, as usual.

The flight from Vegas to Salt Lake City, including the drive to Zable's hotel, took one hour, fifty-five minutes.

Two minutes later the group of men in the hotel room were listening to Keelo's voice on the squawk box.

"... who is this guy anyhow? Rambo? King Kong? Superman! Do bullets bounce off his chest? Does he eat hand grenades for breakfast? Has he got more brains than a Russian chess champion? More moxie than Frank and

Jesse James? Can he say some magic word and turn invisible in the night?"

"What is this shit? He's just one man for Christ's sake—puts his pants on one leg at a time—with two hands—can't hold more than two guns—and you got a whole fuckin' army but he's shooting you down and burning you up. One man making monkeys out of all of you—and *me*—what is this shit!"

There was a pause. Nobody spoke for a moment.

"Are you guys listening? Are you still alive? Or have you turned into a bunch of wax dummies?"

For once Rice had an opportunity to speak "Mr. Keelo, this is Johnny Rice . . ."

"Yeah, what's on that great brain of yours?"

"I just want to remind you," he cast a quick glance toward Zable, then looked away before their eyes could lock, "that I and the boys weren't even here when all that happened last night . . ."

"No shit. Well you're there now, and let me remind you of something else. It was *you* and your fuckin' boys that Mulligan took the money from in the first place. One man—all alone"

"Last night he had help," Rice said. "A driver."

"Well, hell! That *does* make a difference—evens the odds. Who is this driver?"

"We don't know yet," Rice muttered.

"Well find out. Zable?!"

"I'm right here, Mr. Keelo, and before you say another word I'm gonna say something, so listen."

"Go ahead."

"I'm a professional and I consider myself among the best, if not the best. I don't take verbal abuse not even from you. You hired me to do a job and it'll get done—even if you fire me. I'll do it anyhow, because of last night and because of my professional reputation. I am not going to be beat by Mulligan, but I'm not going to waste my time listening to a lot of hot air blowing out of Chicago. Just tell me, you want me to work for you or not?"

"Take it easy, Zable." Keelo's voice was conciliatory without being contrite. "I always said you were the best. Last night was just round one between the two of you. You're in charge and you'll get him. But just so you and the boys know, the one who nails him and gets my money also gets a bonus. Five percent of what's left.

"Now there's a lot of people in a lot of places waiting to see how this turns out. It better turn out right!"

"Mr. Keelo," Rice took a step closer to the speaker, "we're already—"

But Keelo had hung up.

"Shit!" Rice exclaimed.

Zable allowed himself the faint trace of a smirk on his otherwise almost expressionless, poxed face. In front of Keelo's men he had established himself, if not as an equal of the Chicago boss, certainly as an independent contractor, independent enough not to be bunched in with Keelo's stooges whose survival in the business depended on Keelo's sufferance.

Yes, Keelo had blinked, but he was still in command. He still waved that five percent bonus at a band of torpedos who would roast each other or even their mothers over hot coals for a crack at that kind of money and a boost up the Chicago prestige ladder. Particularly if, into the bargain, it meant beating the best. And the best was still Zable—up to now.

Zable wore only a pair of slacks and slippers. He was stripped to the waist except for a Turkish towel semicircled around his sinewy, slightly sloping shoulders. The childhood disease had left his face scarred and pitted, but the rest of his body was smooth and flawless—a compact one hundred seventy five pounds at five feet nine inches.

Zable tugged the towel off his shoulders and tossed it onto an empty chair. "The cops have got his name and description and a hundred witnesses who'll say he was involved in the gunfight at the mortuary. All they know is that he shot first, so they'll be looking for him. I want to find him before they do."

Rice stuck a cigar in his mouth and started to light it.

"Don't smoke that thing in here," Zable snapped.

"Sure," Rice remarked. "I wouldn't want to foul up your room with seven dollars worth of Cuban contamination." And he added, "I still can't believe the cops bought that cockamamie story you dished out."

"Why not? We were just innocent witnesses who were shot at by some maniac, and like good citizens we gave chase at the risk of our own safety."

"With guns blazing?"

"What guns? We were unarmed when the police arrived, but never mind that, I want your people to cover the airport, bus station, and railroad."

"Right." Crago spoke through a bandaged face. His left hand was in a sling. "He left his car there last night. He'll need wheels—or wings."

"He's got wheels," Rice smiled, "remember? You tried to catch him and couldn't. Before I leave and light up this cigar, I'll tell you something else, Señor Zable, if you want to hear ..."

"Go ahead."

"The boys will watch all the avenues of departure from Salt Lake City, but," Rice's smile broadened into a mirthless grin, "I got a hunch Mr. Mulligan isn't going to do any departing until he takes care of," Johnny Rice jabbed the unlit Havana toward Zable, "some unfinished business."

Zable's lapis lazuli eyes turned into slivers of hot ice. "I hope he tries. And if he does, just step out of the way— Mr. Rice."

"You bet I will. You can just bet I will." Rice started toward the door, and the others began to follow.

"Just a minute," Zable snapped. "That driver who picked him up last night, we couldn't make him. You think it could've been that black detective friend of his from Vegas?"

"Positively not."

"Why so positive?"

"Because Detective Lieutenant Bernard Browne was on the plane with us this morning—said he was coming in for the funeral."

"Put a tail on him anyhow," said Zable and walked toward the bathroom.

Chapter 20

Detective-Lieutenant Bernard Browne had called 535-7222 from the Embassy Suites on 600 South and West Temple and had made an early date to meet Captain Sven Olsen of the Salt Lake City Homicide Division in Olsen's office. They had met several times before, until now always in Las Vegas.

Sven Olsen was a huge Viking of a man who could have passed for Merlin's beardless, younger brother. Actually they were distant cousins built along the same Nordic dimensions, with ring fingers the size of bananas and butcher blocks for shoulders. Alone he would have filled a good size closet. He wore a summer-weight short sleeve shirt with a strapped-on shoulder holster harboring a .357 Magnum. Just the sight of him went a long way in restoring a citizen's faith in law and order.

"*God dag, god dag, Ole.*"

"It's good to see you again, Lieutenant." Olsen's voice was deep as ten feet down. "This an official visit or something personal I can do for you?"

"Officially, it's unofficial—not connected with my department. I'm here on my own. But let's say I'd appreciate the same personal and professional courtesy—"

"That you have lavished upon me in the past on several appreciated occasions. You've got it, brother. What's the subject?"

"The subject is murder ... and Mulligan."

"That figures. Do you mind telling me what your connection is with this Mulligan?"

"He's a friend."

"Army?"

"And before, and after. A friend, Ole."

"Okay, but since your friend's come to town he shot a guy, incinerated two more, practically demolished a mortuary, caused a riot—and we're damn lucky two officers weren't killed—all in one night!"

Browne unbuttoned his jacket and sat on the edge of the captain's desk while Olsen paced back and forth leaving little empty space in the room.

"They killed his sister, Ole. Murdered her. Stripped her, and then hanged her like a piece of meat."

There was grim remembrance on Olsen's face. "That's not all they did, Lieutenant. It's my case. I was at the scene. I had to study the pictures. How well did you know her?"

"If I had a sister—"

"Then you don't want to hear about it or see the pictures. Neither does your friend Mulligan. We kept as many of the details out of the papers as we could."

"You got an APB out on Mulligan?"

Olsen nodded. "After what happened last night I've got no choice ..."

"Even if those were the ones who killed his sister?"

"Lieutenant, we're cops, you know that—not judges and juries. He's wanted for questioning. And if he's got many brains, he'll turn himself in. It's the smart—and safe—thing to do."

"Good advice, Captain. I agree with you, and if I run into him at the supermarket, I'll tell him you said so."

"Thanks, Browne. Now what can I do for you?"

"I'll be at the Embassy Suites for a few days. It's your case, but any leads, any breaks, even any rumors, let me know first. Before you move."

"Why?"

"Because he's a friend, Ole."

Chapter 21

The mid-morning summer sun filtered through the tree-covered canyon walls and fingered into the slanting earth, warming it and soaking dry the night juices. Bear River was already a glistening, green-white quicksilver swath rushing to braid with wider waters to the south.

The cabin nearby squatted peaceful and silent, its wood and stone indigenous to the canyon but reassembled to shelter intruders instead of the canyon's natural dwellers.

Mysterious night creatures, such as the owl and the possum and the raccoon, had vanished with the first light, to be supplanted by the chirping and chattering, less arcane denizens of the daylight.

But by night or day the struggle went on. Because in the dark or in daylight there were the creatures that prevailed and those that perished.

There is only one commandment in nature's bible. *Every living thing wants to go on living.* But more often than not, the only way to do that is by killing.

Cat and bird, bird and insect, snake and rodent, fish

and worm, and everything with tooth and claw. All hunters and hunted, few able to store enough for respite from the daily struggle of eat or be eaten, kill or be killed.

But death was not evident in the canyon this cordial mid-summer morning. There were only the sounds and signs of life—and the nearby cabin peaceful and silent from the outside.

On the inside there was the sizzle of bacon and the bouquet of strong coffee in the kitchen where Mulligan stood barefoot and shirtless, wearing only an old pair of faded khaki pants white adjusting the crisping bacon with a deformed spatula.

Abbey Bain was in the main room wearing only a man's shirt, which didn't cover much of her long lovely legs. She stood near the cold, stone fireplace, looking at a picture attached to the tree trunk mantel.

The picture was a photograph of five men, one of them, a three-or-four-years younger Mulligan. The others, including Bernard Browne, were strangers to Abbey Bain. The men were wearing hunting garb and holding rifles. The shot had been taken in front of the cabin. Above the picture there was a hand-lettered sign: THE IDLERS' CLUB.

"Aren't your fellow Idlers liable to show up?"

"What?"

Abbey stepped nearer to the kitchen. "I said aren't your fellow Idlers—those happy-looking hunters in the picture—aren't they liable to pop in on us?"

"Not this time of the season," Mulligan answered from the kitchen.

"What about the police or the fun guys from the mortuary?"

Mulligan entered the main room, still holding the spatula. "Not likely. Place isn't in my name ... Great thunderin' hallelujah!"

"What's the matter?" Abbey turned toward him.

"I've never seen your legs in daylight."

"That makes us even. This is the first good look I've had at your scars."

Last night as soon as they had arrived and embraced, both took off their clothes by the fireplace and Mulligan carried her naked through the moonlit rooms, placed her gently on one of the bunks, and resumed where they had left off at the Great Salt Lake.

They fell asleep, neither remembered when, locked together fiercely at first, then gradually relaxing in seamless sleep that bound them together but severed them from the night world outside.

As usual Mulligan awoke early, disengaged himself from the savorous warmth of her body, showered, and was shaving naked when he heard her voice from the bunk.

"Mulligan."

He wrapped a towel around his midsection and hurried toward the bunk, stopping a couple of feet away as she leaned on a slim white elbow, her breasts full and slanting just above the sheets.

"Right here, Abbey. What is it?"

Her lips altered into a sensuous smile of satisfaction. "Yes, Abbey, there is a Santa Claus, just as sure as there is a Mulligan. It wasn't a dream. It wasn't a fantasy. Abbey, you must have been a good girl this year. What do you think, Mulligan?"

"*Very* good." Mulligan nodded. "Especially the last twelve hours."

"Why thank you, and I can vouch for your excellence

if you ever need an endorsement. In the meanwhile, you may finish shaving and I'll be in shortly to shower."

"You're welcome to come in now. There's plenty of hot water."

"With you around, I don't doubt it. But let's start the day off modestly," she pulled the sheet over her breasts almost to her shoulders, "and work ourselves slowly into an uncontrollable frenzy. Good morning, Captain."

"Good morning, Mate." Mulligan smiled, then turned and walked to the bathroom, still holding the old double-edged razor. "I'll defreeze some bacon and heat up some coffee."

"Coffee's about ready," said Mulligan still looking at her legs stemming from the bottom of the shirt. "And bacon, too."

She started toward the kitchen passing close to him. "Smells good."

"So do you." He put his arms around her, drawing her closer, and kissing her for the first time that morning.

"I've taken two showers," she smiled, "and still can't get the salt out of ... certain places."

He kissed her again. "Want me to try?"

"Coffee's boiling ..."

"So am I. Stand right there."

"What are you going to do?"

"First, something about the coffee," he walked into the kitchen and turned off a burner, "then something about the bacon." He turned off a second burner, and walked back to her.

"And then?" she asked as he kissed her again.

"I'm going to do something about me—us." He unbuttoned the single button that she had fastened on the shirt.

"Why, Captain Mulligan, is this what you consider starting the day off modestly?"

He picked her up and carried her toward the bunk. "I can't help it, my immodesty is beginning to manifest."

"So I noticed. What about breakfast?"

He placed her on the bunk and removed the shirt from her shoulders. "We'll have brunch instead."

"Louise my dear, when next we meet," Browne said into the phone, "be prepared to be kicked in that beautiful, budding butt of yours."

"I quiver at the thought of such violence, especially from a man who is armed and dangerous—unless of course, such an act from said man is a sexual overture."

"Louise . . ."

"Yes, Brownie, what is it this time? Did I forget to pack your talcum powder?"

"No, Louise, but when you made the arrangements at this hotel you said the rooms would be comfortable and the rates reasonable."

"I lied?"

"Sort of. Yes, the rooms are comfortable, two TVs, two telephones, even a basket of booze and fruit and cheese—plus something else."

"What, my dear man?"

"I've just been informed that my stay here is complimentary. Now, Louise, I may just draw a cop's salary, but I can make my way through life without handouts from a certain travel-agency person who is the possessor of a beautiful, budding butt—"

"Listen, Brownie, it's a standard operating business procedure—for every ten suites we book, we get one free. Yours happened to be number eleven—so shut the hell up and go back to being a detective. By the way, good morning and how *is* the detective business?"

"Charming, just like you—and full of it."

"Seen Mulligan?"

"No, but he's torn up the town pretty good, and I've got a feeling he's just getting started."

"You stay the hell out of the cross fire."

"Do I tell you how to run the travel business? Do I stick my nose in your—"

"In my *what?*"

"Never mind. I'll talk to you tonight."

"Grand. Shall I call you or will you call me?"

"I'll call you—collect."

In the gymnasium at the hotel where he was staying, Zable's bare fists beat an incessant tattoo against the punching bag, which was barely visible because of the rapid-fire hammering it was taking from his knuckles. There were bruises on his arms and shoulders from the accident last night, but his proficiency at hitting the bag was not impaired in the slightest.

After a couple of minutes his pattern and rhythm changed, to an even faster tempo.

A black man, broader, taller, and sixty pounds heavier than Zable, wiped the sweat from his face at the end of his workout, stepped three feet to Zable's side, and grinned in admiration. "Man, you sure can make that bag sing."

Zable made no acknowledgment except to step up the staccato *tat-a-tat-tat* of the bag.

The black man shrugged, turned, walked away. His words, "Have a nice day," were snuffled by the buzzsawing bag.

Walter Zable was not a man to be distracted from whatever he was concentrating on, and at the moment he was concentrating on the kangaroo striking bag. Kangaroo bags have been outlawed for years, but that didn't stop certain people from killing kangaroos and using their hides for various adornments, such as shoes, belts, or wallets. Or for striking bags. Zable had no interest in kangaroo shoes, belts, or wallets, but he had a plentiful collection of kangaroo striking bags and took one with him, no matter where he went.

Zable worked out every day, tuning his body and honing his reflexes, a far cry now from the sickly child his coal-miner father had scorned in Nanticoke, Pennsylvania. Partly because Nicholas Zable was a powerful physical specimen, while the child was frail, and partly because Walter's birth had induced his mother's death, Nicholas Zable had no stomach for his son.

So he dug coal, drank, and displayed his physical prowess on every possible occasion, while leaving the rearing of his son to Anna, his homely spinster sister.

Nicholas Zable had only one friend, a strong young miner named Walter. Nicholas even named his son after his friend. But the friendship didn't last long because Walter left the mines and went into college athletics and later professional prizefighting; then he went to war, barely surviving a crash in a bomber he piloted. After World War II he went to Broadway and Hollywood, substituting the name of Jack for Walter. Zable often had seen Jack Palance in the movies and on television, but he had never met the man for whom he was named.

While Walter was still a young child, his father began to dig less coal, drink more whiskey, and brag insufferably at the local bar about his strength. Time after time he bet drinks that no man could hit him in the stomach and hurt him. Time after time he took the blows and won. One time he took a blow and again won the wager, not even wincing. But forty-eight hours later he lost something else. In the midst of swinging an axe toward a wall of coal, Nicholas Zable collapsed and died of an internal hemorrhage.

His father's death seemed to have a salubrious effect on Walter. His health and strength improved perceptibly, and by the time he reached high school he had become a three-letter athlete—track, swimming, and his best sport, baseball. His position was shortstop, and he played it well enough to get a tryout and make the St. Louis farm club. He was a .280 switch-hitter with speed on the bases, a great glove, and a throw to first that fleeced many a runner out of a legitimate hit.

It happened during a scrimmage game with the Cards. One out, man on first, Musial at bat. Double play possibility if the pitcher could get Musial to hit it on the ground. The third baseman barked something at the young shortstop who turned for a second to hear. In that second Musial cracked a searing one hopper that blazed by Zable's glove and crashed into his throat. The impact dropped and almost killed the young infielder. It smashed his Adam's apple, affected his voice box, and ended his athletic aspirations. He tried, but it wasn't like falling off a horse and getting back on. He just could not bring himself to suit up and stand targetlike at shortstop.

Walter Zable would have to do something else.

The idea came to him when he saw a movie with Humphrey Bogart called *The Enforcer,* loosely based on a book entitled *Murder Incorporated.* Everett Sloane played a man named Mendoza who pointlessly kills a stranger in order to prove to his friend that he will never be suspected or caught because of the simple fact that he doesn't have a motive.

Acting on the motiveless-murder theory, Mendoza starts a business. He hires himself out, and then others who work for him, to kill people they don't know because other people are willing to pay money to have the victims dead.

You do not suddenly wake up one morning, finish tying a shoelace, and instantly become a killer—unless you're in a war. Ironically Walter Zable missed out on a couple of wars. He was a year too young for Korea and barely too old for Vietnam. But he probably would have been excused from both involvements because of the damage to his throat.

Watching *The Enforcer* with Bogart broke through the topsoil of Zable's mind and consciousness, but the deadly seed had been implanted in the Slavic roots of some forbear, perhaps one of the cold-blooded Cossacks his father had reveled in bragging about.

Upon reflection Zable realized that ever since his childhood, while watching movies and television he had always been more fascinated, involved, and concerned with the killers in the conflict, rather than the so-called heroes. To this day he bought old movies for VCR and studied the performances and precepts of the classic killers, factual and fictional.

He dismissed the second-string killers played by the likes of Dan Duryea, Richard Conte, George E. Stone, Peter Lorre, Sydney Greenstreet, and Lloyd Nolan. Even farther down the ladder were Barton MacLane, Joe Sawyer, and Steve Cochran, all brutal but low on brains. And then there were the crazies like Jack Lambert, Lee Marvin, and Bob Mitchum in *Night of the Hunter* and *Cape Fear*.

These were not the killers' elite. Those were often played by Robinson, Muni, Cagney, and Raft. At the head of Zable's hit list were two killers portrayed by Bogart and one by Alan Ladd.

In *The Petrified Forest*, Bogart played a secondary character named Duke Mantee, but it was his picture from his entrance to his exit just as sure as he sat there with a tommy gun across his lap and determined everybody's life and death including his own.

The other picture was *High Sierra* where Bogart played public enemy number one, Roy Earle, the last of the Depression-era gangsters whose deadly talent was for hire, but whose code of self-esteem and reliability was unassailable—and incorruptible.

The other classic killer was a man named Raven, acted by Alan Ladd in *This Gun for Hire*. He got fourth billing in the picture, but it made him a star and set off a chain of cinematic imitators who still haven't come close to the genuine article. Even Ladd himself never duplicated the complexity and depth of the Raven character in any of his other criminal or heroic roles.

But as much as Walter Zable identified with and idolized Mantee, Earle, and Raven—studied their mannerisms, moves, and methods, he vowed never to be like them in his chosen profession.

Because each of these men had a professional failing. All of them had the same flaw.

And that flaw was *feelings*.

Mantee waited too long for a woman he trusted. She didn't show up and it cost him his life. The cops would have gotten him sooner or later. But who knows how much later or on whose terms?

Roy Earle wasn't killed by a sniper on the High Sierra Mountain range. He was doomed because of a soft spot he had for a dog named Pard. He should've let the dog chase his car until the mutt dropped dead. Instead he listened to Marie who pleaded with him to take Pard with them. They were traced because of the dog. That soft spot in Roy Earle's heart was what the sniper aimed at and hit.

Raven in *This Gun for Hire* was a solitary, almost silent killer, a paid gunman who dispatched victims without compassion or compunction, but whose failing was a fondness for cats and children—and for Veronica Lake. That parlay inevitably led to his demise.

Ironically the perfect hired killer Zable studied on the screen was played by his father's long-ago friend, the man for whom Walter Zable had been named.

The mercenary killer Wilson. Jack Palance in *Shane*.

Wilson had no feeling—at least none that was betrayed or even divulged. He was immune to emotion. He could kill with a gun in one hand while sopping up gravy with cornbread in the other.

He was laconic, speaking only when it was necessary and effective. Zable could count less than thirty lines spoken by Palance in the picture. Yet he was an impressive physical specimen, with biceps bulging under gartered shirt sleeves.

There was no hint of fealty to family, cause, country, animal, or human. His only loyalty was to himself and to the contract he was paid to execute. And execute was the operative word. He could provoke and slay an innocent sodbuster while the victim's wife and children looked on, then walk through the batwings to finish a drink without taking a deep breath.

This was the consummate killer. With no regard for life or afterlife. A businessman whose stock in trade was tailor-made death. One size fits all, satisfaction guaranteed, results permanent, no strings attached. When the deed was done the doer traveled on to another job site and another piece of work.

This was the character after whom Zable would, and did, pattern himself. There were two primary requisites. One, that he become an expert marksman with a variety of weapons. It took some time and effort but that achievement was relatively easily mastered. The second took more time, effort, and discipline. Zable had to drain himself of every vestige of emotion. There was no place in any corner or crevice of his mind or body for any feeling of friendship, tenderness, sorrow, or sympathy.

He would stop at the site of an accident and view the blood and suffering and death, study the broken bodies and listen to the cries of agony as if he were watching mannequins in storefront windows.

He would attend the funeral of a drowned child whose body lay in a miniature coffin, and while the grieving family broke down, Zable would think of the cold lemonade he would enjoy later that hot summer afternoon.

And he would kill, first cats, dogs, squirrels, and then a few people at random, derelicts mostly—people of little value to society or themselves. Expendables.

Detachment was the key. Friendship was the enemy. And love unthinkable. Curiously, women and sex were not an overpowering drive in his life. From high school on, Zable had had a few fast encounters in front and back seats, all with girls who were more experienced and anxious than he. There were several overnight affairs, almost always at the ladies' lodgings, and almost always after the obligatory performance Zable lay awake until the hour of the morning when he could make sufficient excuse to dress and depart.

For a time Zable feared he had homosexual tendencies, feared it because that, too, would render him vulnerable, but after considerable self-diagnosis, he concluded that he was not homosexual or bisexual. If anything he was closer to asexual or nonsexual. The childhood diseases had affected the growth of his organs and the need that other men found imperative was almost nonexistent in Walter Zable. That made him even more efficient in his newly chosen profession.

But in that profession he couldn't just hang out a shingle like a chiropractor or take out an ad in the Yellow Pages. Somehow he would have to devise a method of making potential clients aware of his ability and availability.

At that time in St. Louis there were two factions vying for control of the city's illicit operations. Both were led by family men, both men churchgoers, and both men careful. One was Victor Mancuso, the other Burt Sturdyvent. Zable didn't care which man succeeded, which failed, so long as he could make his point. After studying the daily patterns of both men, he chose his target.

One morning as was his wont, Mancuso, with his bodyguard, entered the elevator of the building in which he had his office. They were followed by a woman, then a blind man with dark glasses and white cane.

"What floors?" Mancuso inquired.

"Six," said the woman.

"Eight, please." The blind man smiled.

Mancuso pressed six and eight, then Penthouse for his office. The elevator started its ascent.

As they passed the third floor, the blind man produced a gun fitted with a silencer and within two seconds he had shot Mancuso and the bodyguard, both in the head, and had fired a bullet into the heart of the woman who was about to faint. He secreted the gun under his coat and stepped out when the elevator door opened on the sixth floor. There was no one in the hallway. The elevator door closed, and Zable took another elevator back to the lobby, then walked out into the street where sympathetic strangers made a path for the handicapped man.

The murders were never solved. But a month later Zable procured a meeting with Burt Sturdyvent after announcing himself as Monsignor Mahoney. He entered Sturdyvent's office wearing a black suit and white collar.

He then disclosed his true identity and revealed what he had done the month before as Sturdyvent sat agape.

"No charge for that one, Mr. Sturdyvent," said Zable calmly. "But if you or any of your friends have further need of my services, please call this number and leave a message."

Zable put a piece of paper on Sturdyvent's desk and left without another word. Three weeks later, Zable received the first of many calls that sent him on a variety of mercenary missions.

Zable finished working out on the kangaroo bag, showered, and went back to his Salt Lake City hotel room.

Chapter 22

The sun had barely passed its daily high point and begun to arc westward, shifting its heat and light onto the eastern section of the canyon floor.

Mulligan threw a small rock across the river's rushing surface, watching the stone skip three times then disappear beneath the surging water.

He stood near the bank, still wearing the khaki pants but also shoes and socks. Abbey stood near him with the man's shirt tied in a knot around her waist, a denim skirt below it, her feet fitted comfortably into a pair of blue running shoes.

"Damn it, Abbey!" Mulligan picked up another stone and sent it skimming across the river. "Make sense!"

"Last night made sense. So did this morning. Mulligan you said—"

"We both said a lot of things..."

"But you didn't mean them. Is that it?"

"No, that's not it."

"You had a good time but the party's over. Wham, bam, thank you ma'am— or maybe I should thank *you!*"

"Cut it out and listen, Abbey. It's just that if we stay together you're going to get caught in the fireworks."

"You're the one who said they could have gotten my license number or found out who I am."

Mulligan picked up another stone, but this time rubbed it in his palm.

"If they know me," she went on, "they'll find me, like they found Ann."

Through Mulligan's mind's eye there flashed a picture of what would happen to Abbey if they did find her. She wouldn't know where he was, only where he'd been, but that wouldn't matter to them. She had helped him. They would strike back at him through her. Zable, whoever he was, and his associates would find out what they could, then savage her as they had his sister.

"Go to the police," he said, trying to be convincing to her and to himself. "They'll protect you."

"For how long? I could spend the rest of my life in jail, or protective custody. You hear me, Mulligan, the rest of my life! I'd rather spend it with you, no matter what happens."

"Abbey..."

"Look, if you think you've got a better chance to get away without me just say so. Just tell me this is the kiss off, and I'll get out of your way."

"You know I don't want you to go..."

"Then let's leave now—together."

"I can't. Not yet."

"Why?"

"I've got to finish it here, so I can go to another country, with a different name. It can be arranged."

"For both of us?"

Mulligan said nothing. He just rubbed the stone with his palm.

She put her arms around him. "Answer me. For both of us?"

"I think so."

"That's it then." Abbey kissed him. "Mulligan, it's the only choice we've got."

He dropped the stone and put both arms around her, drawing her as close as he could.

Mulligan knew it wasn't the only choice and maybe not the best choice, but if he could work things out with Keyes, it wasn't the worst choice. She had saved his life or at least contributed in tilting the odds heavily in his favor during the mortuary escape. And any one of those bullets could have gone through the back of her head and blown away her beautiful face. In some ways, if his plan to finish off Zable here in Salt Lake City worked, it would be easier to leave the country as a pair rather than alone, since there might be a replacement, or replacements, for Zable.

At the moment he had no specific plan as to how to finish off Zable, or even where to find him. But he had solved other problems, having had fewer specifics to start with.

And if it seemed best for Abbey, at the last minute he would see that she got a wad of dough before he disappeared out of her life. In the meanwhile, maybe because of the excitement, the danger, and the physical attraction, being with Abbey Bain was as close to love as Mulligan could remember.

With her hand in his, they walked together back toward the cabin. Suddenly he grabbed her and pushed her behind a tree.

"Quiet!" he said in a harsh whisper. He had seen a shadow cross a window inside the cabin.

"What is it?" she barely murmured.

"Somebody's inside. Goddammit, I left the gun in there." He looked around for a sign of anyone else outside the cabin, for any vehicle.

Nothing.

Mulligan took her by both shoulders. He spoke low, but there was unmistakable authority in his voice.

"If I'm not out in five minutes, or you hear a gunshot, start running. Here's all the money I've got on me. No matter what happens, don't come back here. You understand?"

"Yes."

"Five minutes. You got a watch?"

"Not with me."

"Take mine." Mulligan undid the band, handed the watch to her, and took off into a wooded area that circled the cabin.

Slowly, silently he made it to the kitchen door. Gently, he turned the knob and inched the door open. It squeaked ever so slightly, but still too loudly.

Mulligan eased in and started across the kitchen toward the door that was ajar. It led to the main room. He stopped, looked around, and spotted a kitchen knife on the sink. Mulligan picked up the knife and proceeded.

There was a faint scraping noise from the main room. Mulligan paused, then proceeded again. His face, at least part of it, looked through the slightly open door.

He saw the back of someone holding his gun, looking out a window. The figure was backlit and his head was stooped.

In a panther move, Mulligan sprang forward, knocked the gun out of the man's hand with a shuto chop, twisted him around violently, and poised the cutting edge of the knife blade at the throat of Detective-Lieutenant Bernard Browne.

In an almost imperceptible beat, each man identified the other. Browne took a deep breath. Mulligan lowered the blade.

" 'Good morning, Vietnam,' " said Browne.

"Bernard, you're slipping."

Browne rubbed his wrist, then picked up Mulligan's gun from the floor and handed it to him. "So are you."

"Yeah, had something else on my mind."

"Might've been a fatal distraction."

Mulligan shoved the gun into his belt. He knew what Browne said was true. It just wasn't like him to make that kind of a slip. He was lucky it had happened under these circumstances, and he would make sure it wouldn't happen again.

"Bernard what're you sneaking around for? Where're your wheels?"

"Somebody put a tail on me."

Mulligan's eyes narrowed.

"I lost 'em. Just the same, I parked on the other side of the road."

"That's a long walk for a flatfoot. When did you get into town?"

"Flew in this morning. Had some interesting company."

"The governor? A senator? Some movie star?"

"Johnny Rice, Louis Lepitino, and half a dozen bell ringers."

"Must be a convention."

"Yeah, and they're out to draft *you*." Browne reacted as the front door opened slowly.

Abbey stood there with one hand on the doorknob and a tire iron in the other.

"I thought I heard voices," she said.

"Come in, it's okay." Mulligan pointed to the tire iron. "What're you going to do with that, Abbey? Fix a flat?"

"Very humorous."

Abbey Bain, this is Lieutenant Bernard Browne— Browne with an *e*."

"Some distraction." Browne smiled.

"Well, well," Abbey glanced at the picture on the fireplace mantel, "one of the happy hunters did pop in on us. You here to hunt wild beasties, Lieutenant?"

"No, I'm here to have some Mulligan stew."

"Sit down, Bernard. If you'll settle for a cup of coffee . . . I'll tell you all about it—you too, Abbey."

Zable was back in his hotel room, wearing Johnston and Murphy loafers, socks that matched his crisp-creased blue slacks, and a freshly ironed white cotton shirt with no tie. Crago stood next to him. Rice, Lepitino, Allen, and Blake also were in the room. If this had been a "best-dressed man" contest Johnny Rice would have taken honors in his Bally shoes, silk socks and shirt, razor-creased summer slacks, Givenchy sport coat, and red Armani tie. But Walter Zable was neither thinking nor talking about wardrobe. "How the hell can you lose a black cop? He sticks out like a raisin in rice pudding."

"We just lost him." Allen shrugged.

"You mean he lost you." He looked at Rice. "What've you got here, a couple of Cub Scouts?"

"They're good men," Rice replied.

"That cop's better. It's a good thing I'm getting some troops from St. Louis. These bums couldn't track a bleeding cat across a white carpet."

"You and your St. Louis hotshots are the ones who lost Mulligan," said Rice.

"Yeah, and I'm gonna find him. When's his sister's funeral?"

"I don't know," Rice answered.

"Well find out."

"You planning on being a pallbearer?"

"Never mind what I'm planning. Just find out and let me know."

"Why don't *you* call?"

"Because I'm telling you to."

"What if they won't tell us?"

"Try. Crago, when are the boys coming in?"

Crago looked at his watch. "A couple of hours."

"Okay." Zable pointed at Allen and Blake. "You two, get back on that cop's ass. You know where he's staying. Sooner or later he's gonna meet up with Mulligan. Maybe he already has. He wouldn't be the first cop that stepped over the line. My hunch is that the two of them are in it together."

"Three," said Rice.

"Three what?"

"Don't forget the driver." Johnny Rice smiled. "There's three of them."

Chapter 23

The three of them—Mulligan, Browne, and Abbey Bain—had drunk two cups of coffee each. Abbey was on her third.

While he talked, Mulligan checked and cleaned several rifles and a couple of handguns that had been stored in a strong container with a heavy lock. The container, bolted to the floor of the main room, had been constructed to pass for a thickly pillowed window seat. Abundant ammunition was also in evidence.

As Browne and Abbey listened, Mulligan recapped the events from the time he'd picked up the man standing beside a disabled Buick, briefcase in hand: the stopover at Flo's, the entrance of two gunmen, the battle, his participation in it, and his escape with a briefcase he soon discovered contained five million dollars in genuine coin of the realm. Browne filled in a few names. Harry Kemp, Artie Lepitino, and Ted Sahadi. He also mentioned that Harry Kemp had knocked off Squeaky Monahan, the other Chicago-bound courier, and that Johnny Rice was under heavy pressure from Chicago to retrieve the contents of the missing briefcase.

Mulligan nodded and continued relating the recent but rapidly occurring events—ditching the Bronco, mailing most of the five million (he didn't mention the destination), buying the Camaro, then finding out about what happened to Annie and calling the mortuary to make arrangements.

He recounted his drive from Tres Cruces to the Croye Funeral Home, where he met Abbey and then four gunsels who represented a killer named Zable, the man who'd murdered Annie. Mulligan glossed over the details of his departure from the mortuary, but emphasized the role Abbey Bain played in his leave-taking and survival.

Before Browne asked the obvious question, Abbey told of her friendship with Annie, of her own terminal illness, and she made it clear that her recent cohabitation with Mulligan was not platonic but passionate, that she intended to stay with him no matter what happened.

Browne barely succeeded in not frowning, but Mulligan could easily sense how his friend felt about involving the lady in whatever was to happen.

There was a momentary silence, then Mulligan spoke. "So except for where I mailed most of the five million, you both know everything from start to ... well, I won't say finish because who knows how it's going to finish."

"I don't want to know where you mailed it," said Browne.

"Neither do I," Abbey added.

"Mulligan," Browne spoke slowly and thoughtfully, "it appears you've got people from Chicago, St. Louis, Las

Vegas and a couple of police departments looking for you—what kind of a *finish* do you expect?"

"Haven't got a worry in the world." Mulligan smiled. "I've got three friends."

"Let me count," Browne reflected. "There's Abbey and me ... that's two. Who else?"

"Somebody in Washington who owes me ... plenty."

"Keyes?"

"Keyes."

"Did you call him?"

"He was out. Should be back today."

"Mulligan." Abbey set down her coffee cup and took a step toward him. "What happens if you give them back the money—or most of it? Make a deal?"

"Are they gonna give me back Annie?"

"I'm sorry." Abbey's eyes drifted toward the floor.

"Look, some money the government didn't know about was on its way to Chicago when somebody pulled a double cross—or was it a triple cross?"

"Don't ask me," said Browne. "I just work there."

"It doesn't matter, because it fell into my lap."

"So did a lot of blood," Browne observed.

"Even if I wanted to, who'd I give it back to? The skimmers? The double-crossers? Or the suckers who lost it in the first place? Who does it belong to? Riddle me that!"

"You're going to get riddled, all right," Browne said.

"If they kill me what have they got?"

"Satisfaction," Browne replied. "Mulligan, they can't let you get away with it! They just can't!"

"What happens," Abbey looked at Browne, "if he goes to the police?"

176

"They might wait till he gets out . . ."

"Or they could send somebody in to do the job," said Mulligan, then addressed Browne. "You know this Zable?"

"Only by reputation. Ba-ad ass."

"He killed Annie. He was probably in that car last night . . . and he's probably still in town."

"Don't even think it!" Browne rose to his feet. "You kill him, they get somebody else."

"Yeah, but I get the one who killed Annie."

"Shit!" Browne turned to Abbey. "Do you have any influence over this maniac?"

"Do I?" Abbey asked Mulligan.

"At times." Mulligan shrugged.

"I wouldn't count on it," Abbey said to Browne.

"And don't count on me!" Browne exploded. "Here's some cheap advice, pal. Get what you have to get from Keyes and then get out of Salt Lake City, out of the country, and, if you can, off this planet—fast!"

"Thanks." Mulligan smiled. "I'll think it over."

"You may not have a whole hell of a lot of time to do that. Well, I'd better be getting back so my tails can spot me again."

"I'll walk you."

"To the car? It's two miles."

"To the fence. It's two blocks."

Mulligan and Browne started to leave, but Browne paused near Abbey Bain. "Abbey, you ought to come with me. Maybe they don't know who you are. Maybe I can fix things."

"There's one thing you can't fix. But thanks." She extended her hand. He held it a moment.

"Yeah. I'm sorry."

Mulligan gave her one of the handguns he had cleaned and loaded. "Stick this in your bustle till I get back. By the way, you know how to use it?"

"My mother taught me." She nodded and Mulligan smiled. Browne didn't catch on, but waved as the two men left the cabin.

While they walked toward the road, Mulligan did most of the talking. "Call the funeral home or, better yet, stop by. Flash your shield, talk to a guy named Edward Croye, Jr. Tell him I had to leave town, but I want Annie buried today. This afternoon. It's the plot next to Tom's. If anyone else inquires, he's to give out absolutely no information, by the way did I say thanks?"

"For what? And you know how I feel about you dragging that girl into this—"

"Yeah, I know. I'll call you at your hotel at exactly six o'clock. Just a couple more things . . ."

Chapter 24

Mulligan attached the battery cables on the hardtop jeep and filled the radiator with water and coolant. The old jeep kicked over as if it had been driven the day before—or the hour before.

Abbey sat in the front seat next to him as he drove toward the gas station and public phone about eight miles from the cabin. This time it was she who jumped out, unlatched the gates, and latched them again after the jeep drove through.

Mulligan, who was not a jabbermouth to begin with, was even quieter than usual. He hadn't said a word since they'd turned onto the secondary road where he'd fired up a Montecruz.

"What're you thinking about?" she finally asked.

"The future," he said.

Mulligan lied. He was thinking about the past and about the man who had become the link between Keyes and him. That man was William Sheppard.

At the time Bill Sheppard was in his early thirties, one

of the transcendent luminaries of the CIA. He was sent to Laos via Vietnam to organize and supervise a covert effort involving thousands of Laotian tribesmen and hundreds of millions of dollars the CIA was spending to provide them with American arms and equipment. Sheppard needed an experienced officer who could help him recruit and train nomadic tribesmen, turn them into a fighting force against the Pathet Lao.

He studied the records of hundreds of officers and interviewed dozens. In the end it came down to Mulligan who had served his original one-year tour of duty and extended in the country for five additional six-month sessions in green hell. Sheppard knew that Mulligan was not a by-the-book officer. He had gone in after his brother-in-law without orders, and on several occasions had acted on expedient impulse rather than wait for a command that might come too late—or not at all. Mulligan's overall success rate was extremely impressive, and the fact that he was still alive was a testament to his ability and to his luck. And this was not to be a by-the-book operation.

So Mulligan went to Laos with Sheppard who became Station Chief there for the CIA. The two of them were responsible for carrying out America's "Secret War." And the two were a curious study in contrasts. Mulligan tense, tight-lipped, and almost frighteningly unemotional; humorless and businesslike in the workplace of war.

Bill Sheppard could have been Errol Flynn in *Objective Burma*, or some other actor playing a part. He reminded Mulligan of Tom Robbins, but he was even more flamboyant, almost carefree in his attitude. Handsome, cheerful, a hero out of books, like Sabatini's Scaramouche, "born with the gift of laughter and the sense that the world was mad."

A study in contrasts they were—but they also were effective in structuring counter-insurgency battalions to hit the Pathet Lao and later divert Vietcong fighting forces from the bloody battlefields of Vietnam to attack the Laotian brigades.

But ultimately the "Secret War" was doomed to failure as was the American "adventure" in Vietnam.

Sheppard was recalled for a time to Washington, and Mulligan went back to just plain soldiering with no connection to covert operations.

In the final weeks before the inevitable collapse of the American campaign, Sheppard surfaced once again in Saigon and once again searched out Mulligan. Not only was the handwriting on the wall, the Cong were on the march. Nothing could prevent the fall of the city. But Sheppard was there to prevent something else.

He had told Mulligan that he was no longer connected with the CIA, but was now attached to the Department of Defense. His assignment, and now Mulligan's: destroy hundreds of millions of dollars worth of American arms, munitions, equipment, and supplies in and around Saigon before the invaders could claim the city and the accumulated glut of a lost cause.

They moved out whatever could be packed into the vessels of sea and air. The rest they blew up in swells of fire and smoke.

In order to get Mulligan assigned to him, Sheppard had pulled a lot of strings. Aboard one of the last planes to leave Saigon, he pulled one more.

"What're your plans for the future?" Sheppard asked.

"Didn't think I'd have a future." Mulligan shrugged.

"Staying in the army?"

"What for?" said Mulligan. "Haven't you heard, the war's over?"

"There're different kinds of wars." Sheppard handed Mulligan a slip of paper. "When you're ready, call this number in Washington. A Miss Fetzer will answer and set up an appointment with a man named Keyes. He's a friend of mine. I told him about you. You two should get together."

Little did Mulligan or Sheppard realize what effect those five words, "You two should get together," would have in the years to come. After spending a month with his widowed sister and arranging to have Tom's body shipped back, and after a monumental weekend drunk with Bernard Browne who had hooked up with the Las Vegas police force, Mulligan called, spoke with Miss Fetzer who arranged for transportation, expense money, and an appointment with Keyes.

During the nearly half-hour interview Keyes did not ask Mulligan a single personal, or, so it seemed, pertinent question. The interview was as bland as Keyes himself. The initials CIA or the word intelligence was never mentioned by Keyes. The whole thing seemed pointless to Mulligan. But then Keyes didn't have to ask Mulligan any questions; he had on his desk a dossier that included more about Mulligan's history than even Mulligan remembered. Finally Keyes rose from his desk, indicating that the interview was concluded, and asked almost as an afterthought if Mulligan would mind spending a few more days in the Washington area.

Mulligan said he would not and, as a matter of courtesy, added that he appreciated the meeting that William Sheppard had set up.

Keyes's reply was the closest thing to a personal observation, and certainly the most surprising declaration, he had made during that half hour.

"Yes, Bill Sheppard is a good man. A very good man. One day he'll be President of the United States."

Mulligan spent that evening with the future President, his beautiful wife, Kitty, and their twin babies, Timothy and Lisa. Mulligan confided to Sheppard that he wasn't all that impressed with Keyes—"Put a jumpsuit on him and he could pass for a meter reader."

Sheppard laughed his usual hearty laugh. "He'll grow on you and vice versa."

"Don't think I'll ever hear from him again."

A week later Mulligan took the CIA exams. A month later he was assigned on a trial basis to the lowest classification on TASK FORCE ELEVEN. A year later he had found out that there were "different kinds of war," and he had risked his life a couple of times for the meter reader.

Mulligan and Sheppard kept in touch, even ran into each other; South America, Spain, England, Iran. Half the time neither could acknowledge knowing the other. Usually Mulligan was under cover, operating under the name Frank Dolan or some other identity Keyes had conceived.

The last Mulligan had heard, Sheppard had been appointed deputy ambassador to Greece and was living in Athens with Kitty and their two children.

Then he heard something else. Keyes called him into his office.

"Bill Sheppard is dead," said Keyes. "Murdered. This morning in Athens."

Why would a deputy ambassador be an assassination

target? Mulligan knew that Sheppard was more than a deputy ambassador. That morning from Keyes he found out how much more. Greece had become the hub of American Mediterranean operations, the home away from home of the Sixth Fleet. The General Staff of the CIA in the Middle East had been moved from Beirut to Athens. This was the center of Intelligence operations reaching out to Turkey, Iran, Libya, Italy, Cyprus, Spain, Portugal, Lebanon, and to other areas vital to American interests. The ambassador was only a figurehead. Sheppard was the strong man who had bargained for and won concessions and cooperation from the Karamanlis government. He was working on a new long-range treaty which would further cement the Greek-American alliance—an alliance that would enhance the American interests and embarrass and unhinge the efforts of the opposition.

William Sheppard had no bodyguard or driver. At ten forty-five the night before, he drove home to the house on Mazaraki Street, parked the Ford in the gated driveway, and started to walk toward the front door. A man stepped out of shadowed bushes and fired twice, directly at Sheppard's head. Kitty had heard the car. She opened the front door just as the shots were fired and saw her husband fall. She was an easy target, outlined in the lighted doorway. The assassin pointed the gun at her for an instant, but instead of firing, he turned and walked away quickly as she ran to the side of her fallen husband.

Sheppard did not die instantly. He lived long enough to whisper the name of his assailant, whom he had recognized as a KGB operative, and to tell his wife he loved her and Timmy and Lisa.

Keyes picked up a dossier marked TOP SECRET and

handed it to Mulligan. "Here's the file on George Rostas, born Gregory Rostov. I guess in the ranks he could be considered your opposite number. We knew who he was and where he was operating, but we never thought he'd— They must have been awfully desperate. If Bill had succeeded, the course of history . . . well, that's a story that'll never be told. I don't understand Rostov's not killing Kitty—everything in his past indicates that he would have and should have. We have to counter. You want the job?"

Mulligan nodded.

"You're the best man I've got, or ever had, Mulligan. But let me tell you this, I know how you felt about Sheppard. This is a job. Don't let your emotions cloud your judgment or change the way you'd do the job. Understand?"

"All right, Keyes, but you try to understand this. Bill and I were in the trenches together. He was my friend. I know his wife and kids. All that probably doesn't matter to you. So I'll do my job, just like it was any other job."

"I know he was your friend, Mulligan," Keyes replied. "He was also my brother."

Mulligan stood speechless.

"My mother was widowed during World War II when my father was killed at Normandy. After the war she married David Sheppard. A year later Bill was born. I kept my father's name, but David Sheppard was the only father I ever knew and Bill Sheppard was the only brother I ever had."

Mulligan managed to mutter "I'm sorry." He took the dossier with him and walked out of the office without looking back.

Just in case they were there, he didn't want to see the tears in Keyes's eyes.

Using the name and passport issued to Gene Bartholomew, Mulligan flew from Dulles International Airport in Washington, D.C., to Heathrow to Athens, took the overnight ferry *Sappho* from Piraeus to the island of Lesbos just off the Turkish coast, rented a car in Mitilini, and drove an hour and a half north to the port of Molyvos. He rented room 305 at the Delphini Hotel which was occupied almost exclusively by German tourists, many of whom had first discovered Lesbos during the Nazi occupation of World War II and now spent vacations on the island taking pictures, enjoying holidays with their wives and children, and reflecting on what might have been.

To escape the German jabbering at the hotel, Mulligan took a taxi and ate at a restaurant in town. Then he took another taxi to Rostas Fishing and Shipping Company where small boats were available for rental. He asked for Mr. George Rostas and was told by a man who worked there—Markos, a short wizened mariner with a white, walrus mustache—that Kirios Rostas, the *effidico*, was unavailable, away on business until the day after tomorrow. Mulligan rented one of the sixteen-foot outboards and paid for three days in advance, plus a healthy deposit, after leaving his name and local residence.

Mulligan asked Markos if he knew of any nearby beaches where the fishing was good, and was told of an isolated cove not far from the hotel where he was staying. Mulligan rented some basic fishing gear and bought bait. He handed Markos a five-dollar tip in American money whereupon the grateful Greek handed Mulligan a Xeroxed map and circled the location of the cove with a ballpoint pen.

Just before he left, Mulligan noticed an assortment of Greek worry beads on a display stand atop a counter.

"How much for a set of worry beads?" he asked Markos.

"Dollars or drachmas?"

"Dollars."

"Two dollars."

"Can they help catch fish?"

"Greek fishermen have used them for centuries."

Mulligan placed two dollar bills on the counter.

"What color?" Markos inquired. "We have green, red, black, white, or blue."

"I'll take the blue to match the sea."

Markos handed him a set of blue worry beads and added, *"Kali tichi."*

"Good luck to you, too," Mulligan replied and left.

Three hours later Mulligan lay on an isolated beach wearing only a pair of swimming trunks. The outboard was anchored nearby. His shirt, pants, shoes, and socks were piled near him on the beach. The rented fishing pole was stuck in the sand, with the line bobbing into the blue water. A Greek sailor's cap shaded Mulligan's face, and a set of blue worry beads was partly tucked into his trunks.

"Mr. Bartholomew?" the voice inquired.

Lazily Mulligan removed the cap from his face and shifted his body, bracing it on his left elbow. "That's right."

He looked at the man who sat on a large rounded rock

five feet away. The intruder was fiftyish, darkly handsome, tanned; with black wavy hair infiltrated by gray, and with olive pit eyes. He was dressed casually and casually held a gun in his right hand, an AMT Automag .22 semi-auto pistol.

"I'm George Rostas."

"Well, Yassoo George. The boat doesn't leak if that's what you were worried about."

"No that's not it." Rostas pointed the gun at the beads dangling from Mulligan's trunks. "And what are you worried about, sir?"

"Nothing in particular. Just picked them up at your place of business." Mulligan held up the beads and smiled.

"I'd say you have a great deal to worry about, *Mr. Mulligan.*"

"In that case I guess I do. You came back from your trip early."

"I wasn't away."

"You could have fooled me."

"That was the idea."

"Then you were expecting me?"

"Or someone like you. I should be flattered that they sent the best."

"It looks like the best wasn't good enough."

"It's ironic. We have so much in common."

"Do we?"

"You have my dossier and I have yours. Both our mothers were Greek. It just happens your father was American and mine ... wasn't. We both served in the military and then intelligence. Once our countries were great allies."

"Yeah, together we beat the Germans, and now they tour our mothers' country and take snapshots."

"Under other circumstances we might buy each other drinks and toast our health. It's too bad we both turned out to be such patriots."

"Is that the gun that killed Sheppard?"

Rostas nodded. "I had to carry out an order. I hoped it would be my last order—until they sent you."

"Why? Are you losing your stomach for murder?"

"Assassination. And you've done your share, as you were ordered. Maybe I am losing my stomach—or something else. The Sheppard incident convinced me."

"Why?"

"He must have lived just long enough to identify me."

"So?"

"So I should have killed his wife. I aimed directly at her heart. A year ago I would have fired without hesitation. I'm not the man I was—and I think they know it. If they don't, they will. But the point is, *I* know it. After this, I might be able to get out."

"I've heard from both sides that we can never get out—alive."

"So have I, but we can try. In a way I'm sorry, *patriotaki*, but you're already out."

"I'm sorry, too," Mulligan held up the worry beads, "that this isn't a rosary."

"A gun would be more useful." Rostas smiled.

"I guess you're right about that too. At any rate, my worries are over." Mulligan looked down at the beads in his hands, snapped the string, and tossed the partially strung beads at Rostas just as Rostas ducked and fired.

About half the beads hit Rostas and exploded inflicting gaping holes in his chest, arms, and legs. The rest of the beads erupted on the shore around him, belching up blasts of sand.

Rostas dropped the gun and fell face forward, bleeding on the beach.

He was dying, but not dead yet.

Mulligan walked to him, stooped, picked up the Automag and fired twice into Rostas'—nee Rostov's—head.

Then Mulligan pulled the anchor rope until the boat was beached. He placed the body inside the outboard and tied the rope, with the anchor still attached, around the dead man. He walked to where his trousers lay, removed from a pocket the blue set of worry beads he had purchased from Markos, walked back to the boat, and stuffed the beads into what was left of Rostas' shirt. The beads were not identical to but a close facsimile of the string he had brought with him to Greece.

Mulligan turned the bow of the boat seaward, got in, started the motor, fired two shots into the hull below the water line, shifted the lever into gear, jumped out, and watched the vessel head toward the open sea. At the rate the boat was cutting through the water, it might cover two or even three miles before it sank to the bottom, taking its cargo along with it.

He flung the gun as far as he could into the cove, dressed, and started to walk in the direction of the Hotel Delphini. As he came closer to the hotel he saw a herd of goats.

The goat at the head of the herd had a bell strung around his neck which sounded as he walked. The rest of the goats followed the leader and the sound of the bell.

The next night Mulligan slept in Washington, D.C., after calling Keyes and telling him the job was done.

* * *

And now Mulligan was about to call Keyes again—and to call in a marker. If Keyes went along, then he and Abbey had a prayer of a chance. If Keyes refused, all they had was a past.

Mulligan stopped the jeep close to the public phone just outside the gas station. He started to get out. "Well, come on." He motioned to Abbey.

"Isn't this a private call?"

"We've got nothing private from each other, not anymore."

Mulligan dialed the coded number.

"Hello," Miss Fetzer answered.

"This is Argonaut."

"Hello, Argonaut. How are you?" The question and the touch of concern in Miss Fetzer's voice were unlike her unusual answering-machine inflection and attitude.

"I'm okay. Is he there?"

"Just a moment, I'll get him off of the other line."

Five seconds.

"Hello, Argonaut." If Miss Fetzer's voice had betrayed a hint of anxiety, Keyes's did nothing of the kind. He might as well have been greeting his gardener or the gas-station attendant.

Mulligan wasted no words in salutation.

"It's the last marker. L-D. Need five M in Cs. Q—tonight. S-L-C. You know the spot—midnight."

"Tonight?" Keyes repeated.

"Tonight. Bring Frank Dolan. By the way, there's a *Mrs.* Dolan. First name—Laura."

"Stats?"

Mulligan looked at Abbey. "Age twenty-eight . . . height 5 feet six inches . . . weight one hundred twenty four."

"One-two-*oh*." Abbey mouthed and circled her thumb and forefinger.

"Make that one-twenty," said Mulligan, "and make her blond. We'll provide the photo."

"Anything else?"

"A K-kit."

"Figures. I could get fired, and you could get killed."

"They wouldn't fire you. You know too much."

"So do you. See you, Junior." Keyes hung up.

So did Mulligan, with obvious relief and even glee. "Holy shit! He went for it!" Mulligan flipped away the butt of the Montecruz.

"Went for what? I appreciate your letting me in on your private conversation, but what language was that? Semaphore? Swahili? Spyski?"

"Survival." Mulligan gave her a private-type kiss in public. "I'll bet you look great as a blonde."

He put an arm around her shoulder and started to walk back toward the jeep. As he did he thought to himself that that was the first time Keyes had ever called him Junior. Could it be that the meter reader was beginning to feel fatherly toward him?

Mulligan dismissed the thought. Keyes had only one offspring—TASK FORCE ELEVEN. But then again, Mulligan was a part of that family—or had been. He remembered his conversation with Rostov at Molyvos and wondered can you ever really get out ... alive?

What good did it do to wonder?

Chapter 25

The Fleur-de-Lis French Beauty Shoppe was located on Beck Street at the north end of Salt Lake City. The proprietress whose baptismal name was Irene Swiderski maintained that she was French on her mother's side. She was considerably overweight on both sides.

Irene personally supervised the blonding of Abbey Bain.

"You're gonna love this," Irene remarked as she cracked her chewing gum—she was trying to quit smoking again. "And so are the men in your life."

"*Man.*" Abbey smiled.

That man was inside Maury's Western Apparel Corral looking at male and female mannequins appareled in genuine dude-ranch outfits.

"Welcome, pardner," said Maury himself, looking Mulligan up and down. "I'd say forty-two long ... thirty-five waist, sixteen and a half shirt. Size twelve boot."

"Bull's-eye," Mulligan replied.

* * *

He walked into the Fleur-de-Lis French Beauty Shoppe where he had dropped her off earlier. But now he wore a typical Western wardrobe—circa late 20th century—including imitation Stetson but genuine Porsche Design sunglasses. Mulligan carried a large cardboard box and a lady's Western hat box both labeled Maury's Western Apparel Corral. He stopped and stood facing the mirror reflecting his image and Abbey's beautiful, newly blond hair, dyed, dried, and being combed out by Irene.

"Howdy, Tex." Abbey smiled.

"Howdy, ma'am," Mulligan replied.

Irene looked from the mirror image of Mulligan to the man himself, appraised him for about a heartbeat, then winked at Abbey. "I see what you mean," she said, while cracking her chewing gum.

Lieutenant Bernard Browne stopped by the Croye Funeral Home—what was left of it—and, after displaying his shield, spoke to Edward Croye, Jr., who showed much more sangfroid and much less bleakness than would have been expected in the wake of last night's events and the attendant wreckage.

Either Mr. Croye was being philosophical or else he was heavily insured. Even though the conversation didn't last long, by the time it was over Browne would have bet on the latter. After promising to comply with Mr. Mulligan's request, Croye mentioned that the funeral home would stay open during remodeling and handed Browne a business card, "Just in case." He added with warm assurance that Mr. Mulligan's deceased sister's body had escaped the blaze and remained serene and beautiful.

Browne stuck the Croye Funeral Home business card in his shirt pocket and started to leave, but asked one more question. "Has anyone called inquiring about Mrs. Robbins' funeral?"

"No, sir."

"If anyone does call, you are to give out absolutely no information. Not to anyone. Do you understand?"

"Yes, sir."

As Browne started to leave again, the phone rang. Browne kept going.

"Croye Funeral Home. Edward Croye, Jr., speaking. How may I be of help?... The Ann Robbins' funeral?"

Browne parked the rented Ford Escort, which was too small for his frame, in the Embassy Suites parking lot and walked into the lobby.

After he had entered and taken a few steps, Browne saw Johnny Rice and Louis Lepitino appear on either side of him. Evidently they had dismissed the tails he had recognized from the flight and had decided to take a more direct approach. Browne decided to find out from them whatever he could. "How you doing, gentlemen? This is a coincidence. You staying here?"

"No," said Rice. "We're at the UT-HO. You on duty, Lieutenant?"

"Nope."

"Buy you a drink?"

"Yep."

Browne, Johnny Rice, and Lepitino sat at a table in the private club which in most any other state would be called the hotel bar. Each of them drank tonic. Rice and Lepitino's tonics were laced with vodka. Browne's was joined with gin.

"Okay, Lieutenant, let's skip all the talk about how ducks make love and the other bullshit and get down to business."

"Go ahead."

"Speaking of business, you know that's what I am. A businessman, not a hit man."

"Like Zable?"

"Those are your words, not mine, and how do you know about Zable?"

"In business there's such a thing as 'quid pro quo'—so far all you're doing is asking questions."

"Okay, you tell me what you know and I'll do the same."

"Zable hit Ann Robbins. He missed Mulligan. I'd say he's still in town."

"He's staying at the same hotel we are. Where's Mulligan?"

"At the moment I don't know."

"But at some other moment, you might?"

"*Quién sabe?*"

"Tell him I've got a deal for him."

"A deal he can't refuse?"

"A deal he *shouldn't* refuse."

"Let's hear it."

"Tell him he can keep five percent as a 'finder's fee.' I'll square it."

"If I did talk to him, why would he be persuaded to do such a thing? He already has one hundred percent."

"To keep on living. I'm his life insurance."

"What about Zable?"

"He's just a hired hand, temporary help. I can cancel

out Zable, *if* Mulligan deals with me. Will you tell him that?"

"If I talk to him I'll tell him, but . . ."

"But what?"

"He's stubborn." Browne shrugged. "Irish, you know."

"Don't Irishmen want to live?" Rice took a swallow of vodka and tonic. Lepitino did the same.

At another part of the bar, Crago, who had removed the sling from his left arm, sat, unable to hear the conversation between Browne, Rice, and Lepitino but watching as the three men sipped their drinks and conferred.

Rice was doing his sincere best to cap the closer on the deal. "But he's got to move fast. Zable's got more troops coming to town."

"When?"

"They're probably already here. And, Lieutenant, they'll be watching you."

"No shit."

Historic Temple Square, 50 West South Temple is the symbolic heart of the worldwide Church of Jesus Christ of the Latter-day Saints. The square is completely enclosed by a 15-foot wall and contains the imposing granite Temple, the dome-shaped Tabernacle with its great organ, information centers, the Assembly Hall, the Temple Annex and the Seagull Monument. Tours of the Tabernacle are offered at 15-minute intervals.

Mulligan and Abbey were among the tourists being guided through the mammoth Tabernacle. And many of them were dressed in the same style, neo-Western garb.

Either Maury was doing a boomtown business, or else there were a lot of other establishments specializing in West-about wrappings.

A multitude of male and female voices, belonging to members of the Mormon Tabernacle Choir, rang out in rehearsal of that group's most famous offering, "The Battle-Hymn of the Republic." "Mine eyes have seen the glory of the coming of the Lord ...' "

"Isn't this ... dangerous?" Abbey whispered to Mulligan as she looked at all the people surrounding them.

"Remember Edgar Allan Poe's 'Purloined Letter'?"

"Vaguely."

"Sometimes the best place to hide is in the open."

"I know a better place to hide."

"Where?"

"Under the covers." Abbey smiled.

Mulligan looked at his watch.

"By George," he said, "I do believe we've got just about enough time to duck for cover." He took her by the hand and broke away from the troop of tourists as the chorus achieved it's triumphal climax: " 'Glory, Glory Hallelujah! His truth is marching on!' "

At the moment it didn't make any difference to Browne whether or not he was being tailed. He stopped at Homicide and dropped in on Captain Sven Olsen.

"You ever hear of a guy named Zable? Ba-ad ass. Very bad."

"Heard of him. Walter Zable."

"He's in your fair city."

"Is there a law against that?"

"You think he's here to visit Symphony Hall?"

"I wouldn't know."

"Would you know if he was involved in an automobile accident the night the mortuary was touched off?"

"Not my department."

"Do you mind if I check with the proper department?"

"Help yourself."

"You got a file on Walter Zable and his known associates?"

"Yep."

"Can I check that out?"

"Help yourself."

"You know what would be interesting, Ole?"

"What?"

"To find out if Walter Zable was in your fair city when Ann Robbins was murdered. He's stopping at the UT-HO. Sorry I don't know the room number."

Mulligan and Abbey were not under the covers, but they were back in the cabin, naked and deep in the act of making love. Mulligan was not completely naked. He wore his watch. As subtly as possible he glanced at it and accelerated his body motion. "Honey, I've got to hurry or I'm gonna be late."

"Then go ahead and hurry, big boy," she breathed. "I'm dancing as fast as I can."

Browne was on the phone in his hotel room, glancing at his watch. "Just like the 'B and O,' Mulligan. Always on time."

"Old army habit. Anything?"

"Yeah, Rice says he'll fix it for you to keep a five percent 'finder's fee' if you turn in the balance."

"Generous. What does Zable say?"

"Nothin', but his main man was tailing Rice or me—or both of us."

"A big muhuska?"

"Yeah, I mugged him at headquarters, name's Crago."

"We met at the mortuary."

"I also sicced homicide on Zable in connection with Annie."

"A lot of good that'll do. Where's Zable staying?"

At the UT-HO. But you stay away. He's got plenty with him. You hear?"

"I hear."

"You talk to your third friend?"

"He's coming through. Midnight tonight. Right here in town."

"Then that's a good time for you to leave Salt Lake City."

"Just like the 'B and O,' Bernard, I always pull out on time."

Chapter 26

The summer sun had disappeared beneath the Salt Lake City skyline half an hour ago. The hardtop jeep was parked with the windshield facing the entrance of the UT-HO. Abbey sat behind the wheel, Mulligan slouched in the passenger seat with the counterfeit Stetson pulled low across his brow. Both were still outfitted by Maury except for Abbey's hat. She refused to wear it and left it at the cabin saying it was too heavy and besides it made her look like a road company Annie Oakley.

Mulligan's grunt, at that time, could have signified agreement or disapproval. In either case Abbey didn't care, she still left the hat behind.

" 'Oh, vanity,' " Mulligan muttered from under his hat, "thy name is woman.' "

"What the hell is that?"

"I'm not sure. It's a part of a poem or epigram or essay."

"No, I mean what's it supposed to mean and why did you just say it?"

"Because I just figured out why you didn't want to wear that hat."

"I already told you why."

"Horsefeathers. I know the real reason."

"Let's hear it, oh great occidental philosopher."

"Because you look so beautiful in your new blond tresses you don't want to hide them. Vanity. Pure and simple."

"Mulligan, you know what . . . ?"

"Yeah, I know what." The tone in Mulligan's voice changed. "If that big guy second in line is Crago—and it is—then the point man must be Zable."

They were just coming out of the hotel entrance. Besides Zable and Crago there were three others from St. Louis—Pryor, Raskin, and Bevo. They made their way toward a Lincoln Town Car. The thought came to Mulligan that after the smashup, the Cadillac rental company probably preferred not to do further business with the destructive duo.

Crago had recovered sufficiently to act as driver again. Zable took his place in the front seat and the remaining three squeezed into the rear. It was a squeeze since none of them weighed less than two hundred and twenty pounds.

The Lincoln moved west to Main Street, turned right and proceeded north. So did the jeep.

"Why don't you get out and go to a movie? I'll pick you up later."

"I've been to a movie."

"Not too close."

"What?"

"Don't get too close."

Mulligan pointed to the Lincoln ahead. "I'm talking about the car."

"Mulligan you're getting too bossy. Next time I'm getting on top. Got that?"

"Yes, ma'am." Mulligan nodded. "Equal rights and equal nights."

The sign said, THE AMBASSADOR—Private Club.

The club was done with much wood and brass, black and red leather booths, black and white tile floor, and a tall ceiling.

The room was less than half full. Zable, Crago, and the others had been seated at an "A" booth midway between the kitchen and the entrance. They had been served their first round of drinks and were glancing at oversized menus. The others had ordered scotch, vodka, gin, and bourbon. Zable seldom drank anything except Coca-Cola and never consumed alcohol when he was on a job.

"I think you were right," said Crago, bending the menu on the table, "Rice is trying to pull a fast one. Him and Lepitino looked awfully chummy with that Las Vegas cop."

"I'll have a talk with our two chums later tonight or tomorrow morning." Zable nodded at Pryor, Raskin, and Bevo. "Another drink, boys?"

"Yeah, sure," said Pryor, swallowing the last of his scotch and water. "I thought Salt Lake City was dry."

"There's more booze here," Zable noted, "than there is beer in St. Louis."

"That reminds me," Crago rose and placed his menu and napkin on the seat of the booth, "I got to go to the can. Somebody order me another jolt, huh?"

He walked toward the rear of the dining room, past the double kitchen doors, and headed for the sign marked Rest Rooms with an arrow pointing in the direction of a hallway. Crago moved past the first ornate entrance with the hand-lettered gold-leaf sign, Women, to the second ornate door separated by two public phones and lettered Men.

He pulled open the heavy door and entered. As the door barely closed behind him, he absorbed a fast, hard shuto blow to his throat from the edge of Mulligan's hand.

Crago was stunned; he wobbled and would have fallen, but Mulligan grabbed him with both hands, slammed him against the wall, and braced him there.

"Do you know who this is?" he asked in a harsh voice. "I want you to know it's Mulligan. Ann Robbins' brother."

Mulligan again slammed him against the wall. "Got that? Ann Robbins' brother."

Crago's eyes seemed to find focus. He barely nodded.

Mulligan slapped then backhanded Crago across the jowls. Hard.

While Zable, Pryor, Raskin, and Bevo were finishing their second round of drinks, Crago's still remained untouched.

"I'm gettin' hungry," said Pryor. "What the hell happened to him?"

"Maybe he fell in." Raskin smiled.

"He's got hemorrhoids real bad." Bevo smiled wider. "Maybe he's bleeding to death."

"I've got to to anyhow." Zable rose. "Too much Coca-Cola. Go ahead and start ordering; I'll be right back."

Zable followed the route Crago had taken. He reached the rest-room door, opened it, and went through. "Hey, Crago, what the hell . . ."

That was as much as he said.

From a brass crosspiece above the toilet stall, Crago was hanging by the rope around his neck, twisting naked. At first his bare back was to Zable, but then slowly his hairy body revolved, revealing dead rasberry eyes bulged open—a hundred-dollar bill stuffed into his mouth.

Crago had defecated on the rumpled pile of clothes on the toilet floor beneath him, and blood still dripped from his rectum.

Chapter 27

The jeep, which had been parked half a block down the street from the Ambassador, pulled away from the curb with Abbey at the wheel while Mulligan resumed his slouch on the passenger seat.

"What were you doing in there?" she asked.

"Just . . . hanging around," Mulligan replied and looked at his watch. "We're pretty much on schedule, mate. Turn left at the next light."

"Do I get to sit in on the meeting with whatshisname?"

"What would be the point?"

"The point is I get lonely waiting around in this crate. It smells of fish and dead meat. Mulligan, am I beginning to smell like fish and dead meat to you?"

"You smell like a gardenia."

"I don't like gardenias."

"Then you smell like an orchid."

"Orchids don't smell. You're not good at botany, better stick to anatomy."

"You might live to regret that statement."

"I certainly hope so."

Immediately Mulligan regretted his own statement about "living" but if Abbey was distressed she showed no sign of it."

Damn, Mulligan thought.

The meeting took place at the Saltaire Palace on Salt Lake Island, where Mulligan and Keyes had met on two other occasions when it had been imperative that Mulligan not be seen in Washington.

Keyes had arrived first and was sitting on a bench as Mulligan approached and sat next to him.

Keyes's attitude was as casual as if he had just stepped across the hall from his office instead of having flown two thousand miles in a company plane to rendezvous with an ex-spook at two o'clock in the morning Washington time. His suit, shirt, and tie looked as if they had been laid out by a butler fifteen minutes ago. Not a solitary strand of hair strayed out of place.

Maybe Keyes was a cold, hard man in a cold, hard business, but tonight he looked to Mulligan like a guardian angel risking his wings to come to the rescue of a falling sparrow.

"Hello, Mulligan."

"Hello, Keyes."

"Miss Fetzer sends her regards. As usual she was fructuous in putting this little package together within the time frame you designated."

"Tell her I said thanks. So it's still *Miss* Fetzer, huh? When's that dame ever going to get married?"

"I don't know. Maybe *you* should have asked during that weekend."

"So you knew about that, too. Does she know that you know?"

"No, and I shouldn't have mentioned it. I would appreciate it if you never told her I did."

In Mulligan's memory, that was as close to self-reproach as Keyes had ever come. It was unusual that he had brought up Miss Fetzer's name at all. Maybe this was his way of saying that he had hoped she and Mulligan would have gotten together on a more permanent basis. But Mulligan wasted no more time analyzing Keyes's motivation as far as Miss Fetzer was concerned.

"Don't give it a thought, Keyes. Odds are I'll never see or talk to her again—or you."

Keyes snapped open a briefcase revealing stacks of hundred-dollar bills face up.

"Ben Franklin," said Mulligan. "My favorite printer." He picked up a hundred-dollar bill and rubbed it between his thumb and forefinger. "Say, Keyes, this stuff looks damn good."

"It ought to look *familiar*. It's the same queer you used down in Nicaragua."

"What're you doing, recycling?"

"Why not?"

"Not this time. This might go blowing in the wind. Okay?"

"Okay." He shrugged. "We've got plenty more." Keyes handed over a passport opened to a photograph of Mulligan. "Here's Frank Dolan."

"Greetings, Frank."

"And Mrs. Dolan." Keyes produced another passport with a missing photo. "Don't I get to meet her?"

"She asked the same about you. Best you don't."

"That's all right. I'm not even here. There are eleven witnesses who'll swear I'm at a weekend party in Virginia."

"Only eleven?"

"One's the Vice President and two are cabinet members."

Keyes brought forth a five inch by seven inch leather box two and a half inches deep. He opened it, revealing five capsules lying in five depressed molds along with a contracted aerial. Next to each mold, a tiny button. "Here's the kit. They're set for six seconds."

"Good."

"Don't let 'em go off in your pants."

"Not *my* pants. C-4?"

"C-6." Keyes replied.

"What happened to 5?"

"A chemist type fellow made a slight miscalculation. Went off in *his* pants—so to speak."

"Keyes, this squares us." That was as close to saying thanks as Mulligan came.

"Maybe. I'm sorry about Annie."

"Yeah."

"Don't know what you're up to but—"

"I know. You never heard of anybody named Mulligan—or Dolan."

Keyes rose and started to walk away. "Take care of yourself, Junior."

Chapter 28

Holding the briefcase in one hand and the K-kit and passports inside a tote bag in the other, Mulligan waited just over a minute until Abbey turned the corner and stopped in front of him. Rather than park in one spot, Mulligan had told her to keep moving and pass by the corner every four minutes. Knowing Keyes, Mulligan figured: A) He would be on time; B) The meeting would not take long. Right on both counts. As Abbey reached across and opened the door, Mulligan hopped into the jeep. He settled onto the passenger seat, set the briefcase between his legs, and slammed the door shut.

"I see your date showed up." She nodded toward the paraphernalia Mulligan brought aboard.

"Never a doubt. What do you feel like?"

"Do you have to ask?"

"Thought you might want to stop for a steak—or a pizza."

"Let's stop for nothing."

Mulligan pointed ahead as the jeep pulled out. "You know the way."

"Ah, yes. 'Let me count the ways'—that's poetry, my man."

"And so are you."

"Whatever is in those bags must be awfully important to have your scoutmaster fly all the way out here—and back I presume. Now I heard your telephone conversation, but it made as much sense as Chinese music. So let me guess, they *don't* contain pizzas—or steaks."

"Right."

"See, I'm brilliant."

"And beautiful. Permit me to interpret said telephone conversation."

"Now Mulligan I wouldn't want to break any scout rules ..."

"You're in our troop, don't you remember the initiation?"

"I was hoping it wasn't over yet."

"We're working on merit badges now—let's see what the hell did I say to him? Oh, yeah. 'The last marker'— the last favor he owes me and I need to collect. 'L-D'— life or death, mine and yours. 'Need five M'—that's five million. 'In Cs'—that's C notes, hundreds. 'Q' stands for queer money, counterfeit. 'Tonight'—that means tonight. 'S-L-C.' Salt Lake City. 'You know the spot'—we met here twice before. 'Midnight'—always in the time zone you're calling from. 'Bring Frank Dolan'—that's a ready-made passport and identity I've used before. 'Mrs. Dolan ...' " He held up the second passport. "This one's brand new, made up this afternoon. All we've got to do is plant your pretty blond picture on it—simple?"

211

"As Chinese music ..."

"And the K-kit ... well, let's just let that be the pièce de résistance."

"There you go with sex again—I'm not complaining mind you, matter of fact I'm driving as fast as I can."

"Don't drive too fast. Some cop may not have made his quota for the night."

"I won't say it." Abbey Bain slowed the jeep just a little bit.

But Mulligan was still thinking like a spook. When he'd said to Keyes "This squares us," Keyes had replied "Maybe." Did that mean Keyes still owed Mulligan? Or Mulligan still owed Keyes? If it meant the latter, someday Keyes might want to collect. Mulligan knew he would pay off—if the boy scout survived the Salt Lake City expedition.

Inadvertently Mulligan's fingers squeezed a little tighter on the tote bag containing the K-kit.

After they turned off the secondary road and drove toward the cabin, it was Mulligan's turn to do the hopping in and out of the jeep, the unlatching and latching of the gates. If it is possible to whistle and smile at the same time, then that's what Mulligan was doing. Part of the time he whistled tunelessly, and sometimes he slid into a reasonable facsimile of "Something to Remember You By."

"Mulligan, what in hell is the name of that song you're trying to whistle?"

" 'Please Give Me Something to Remember You By.' "

"Before my time."

"Written by Schwartz and Dietz—would you rather I *sang* it to you?"

"I don't think so, but it's good to see you smile. In all the years I've known you, I haven't seen you smile this much."

"Yeah, and we practically grew up together. Why shouldn't I smile? I've got five million dollars between my knees and my girl by my side. You are my girl, aren't you?"

"Yes, Mulligan, I'm your girl. But you do realize that money isn't real, don't you?"

"What the hell is?"

She parked the jeep under the porte cochere. He handed her the key to the cabin, hefted the briefcase and tote bag, and they walked toward the front door.

"Don't forget," she said, "I'm on top."

"You can start out that way, but after a while I just might flip you for it."

"Promise?" Abbey unlocked the door and pushed it open. "Mulligan, you know what?"

"What?"

"You already have."

"I already have ... *what?*"

"Given me something to remember you by."

She walked through the doorway and Mulligan followed.

He walked into a big fist that burst against the side of his jaw and nearly knocked him off his feet.

Immediately, Lieutenant Browne slammed the door shut and hit a light switch. Abbey was about to leap upon Browne when the light went on. Mulligan had dropped both bags and was shaking some sensibility into his brain.

"Bernard," Mulligan said. "Is this a test?"

"No. It's for making me an accessory to murder." He pointed at Abbey. "And her too."

"What's he talking about?" Abbey asked Mulligan.

"I'm talking about what happened at the Ambassador Club tonight," Browne answered. "You don't know that Crago got killed?"

"I thought that was suicide." Mulligan's fingers pressed against his jaw.

"Yeah, right after he took off all his clothes and stuffed a hundred-dollar bill in his mouth, he hanged himself."

"Maybe his conscience caught up to him."

"No, you did."

"I was nowhere near the joint." Mulligan looked at Abbey. "Was I?"

"What joint?" she asked ingenuously.

"It was murder, Mulligan."

"Justice," he replied. "If you had been there you—"

"I *was* there. My friend from Homicide called."

"That was friendly. Did your friend from Homicide ask Zable about Annie?"

"Yeah." Browne nodded.

"And?"

"Well..."

"Let me guess. At the time Annie was murdered, Zable was pitching pennies with a priest, a rabbi, and a Baptist minister. Right?"

"Something like that," Browne conceded. He glanced at the briefcase. "Did Keyes come through?"

"One hundred percent."

"Then leave, *tonight!*"

"Can't. I got a date."

"With a coffin."

"Maybe a lot of coffins, tomorrow at CopperScott."

"Look Mulligan, we've gone up against odds before, plenty of times, but—"

"Don't give me any of that 'we' shit. This is my business and my ass. Not yours," he waved toward Abbey, "and not hers. When I go up against 'em it'll be alone. And I don't need you to tell me what's right and what's wrong, or to walk across my grave before I'm dead. So beat it, Bernard. Just blow!"

"I'll beat it all right. Because you know what, Mulligan? You're fucking crazy!" Browne stormed out, slamming the door behind him.

The moon, full and egg-yolk yellow in the waterless sea of deep blue sky, floated like a becalmed balloon. The canyon and its living creatures breathed the cool and anodizing night air, and the creatures blinked back at the shimmering planets and the eternal stars.

Mulligan lay in the bunk, his head on a couple of pillows. He was covered by a sheet from his bare waist down, and he rubbed his jaw. He could hear the sound of running water from the bathroom sink. Then the water was turned off.

Abbey emerged carrying a dampened face cloth. She wore only a towel, sarong-style, that enwrapped her body from her breasts to her thighs.

She walked across the moon-splayed room, through the shadows, and stopped at the side of the bunk, facing Mulligan. She stood close. Very close. She leaned over and placed the cloth on Mulligan's face.

"Does it hurt?"

"Does what hurt?"

Mulligan reached up and untucked the towel from Abbey's breast.

The towel fell and she stood naked.

She shifted her body slightly, and as she did the moonlight met her upper thigh and illuminated the tattoo of a small butterfly.

Mulligan guided her onto the bed with him.

As they made love the butterfly seemed to be alive—undulating, pulsating, trembling—and finally as Abbey sobbed and kissed Mulligan fiercely, the butterfly ceased its moving.

Chapter 29

"Brownie, I just love hearing the sound of your voice, especially in the middle of the night. I just wish it weren't over the telephone. There's a nice big empty spot on the bed right next to me."

"It won't be empty long."

"Good. Is everything okay?"

"Everything stinks."

"Mulligan?"

"Mulligan."

"Is he alive?"

"Not for long. Louise, he's gone fucking crazy and nothing I or anybody else can say or do'll bring him to his senses. He killed somebody else tonight and tomorrow there's going to be a slaughter including him. He told me to blow."

"And what are you going to do?"

"I'm coming home."

"Home? I like the way you say that . . ."

"I'm going to say something else when I get there. I've

been thinking, Louise, mostly about you and me. Maybe it's this Mulligan business—or maybe I've finally come to my senses—but I don't want to walk without you baby."

"Bern ..."

"But we've got to talk a few things out."

"We'll talk ..."

"I'm a cop and I'm going to keep on being a cop, not some goddamn sugar-coated travel agent. You've got to accept that ..."

"I accept, I accept."

"And I'm not going to live off your money and start shitting in high cotton. Got that?"

"I got it! You don't have to say anymore."

"I've got plenty more to say, but it can wait 'til I get there."

"I can't wait. When, Bern? I'll pick you up ..."

"No you won't. I'm not sure when. But it'll be tomorrow, and I'll fill up that empty spot. Just wait there for me. Don't go to work."

"It's Sunday!"

"So it is."

"Bern, I wish something could be done about Mulligan."

"So do I. But it's too late for him. I don't want it to be too late for us. I love you, Louise."

"I love you, Brownie. Good night—I mean good morning."

As Browne hung up, there was a knock on the door. He walked toward it, checked his watch for the time, and unsnapped the strap of his holster. "Who is it?"

"Johnny Rice, Lieutenant. Got to talk to you."

Browne opened the door. As usual Louis Lepitino stood half a step to Rice's side.

"What're you doing?" Browne said. "Delivering milk?"

"I know it's late, but this won't take long ..."

"Come in, come in."

Rice and Louis entered, and Browne closed the door behind them.

"Been trying to reach you. First there was no answer, then your line was busy so we came over. Left you a couple of messages ..."

"Yeah, well I've been a little busy, and I'm about to go to bed so what can I do for you in ninety seconds?"

"Zable called. He wants to see me in the morning ..."

"So?"

"So we heard what happened to Crago ..."

"And?"

"Did you talk to ... to Mulligan?"

"Yeah."

"What happened?"

"I did more than talk to him. I tried to beat some brains into his skull. It didn't work, Johnny. It's no deal. He's gone bananas."

"He killed Crago, didn't he?"

"What do you think?" Before Rice could reply, Browne continued. "I'll tell you what I think. I think this climate is unhealthy. I think there's going to be an epidemic starting tomorrow, and I'm getting the hell out of here. If you've got the sense of a warthog, you'll get out, too, let whatever happens happen, and pick up whatever chips are left on the table."

"I can't. I got people to answer to."

"In order to answer, you've got to be able to talk. In order to talk, you've got to be alive. Just ask Crago."

Rice looked at Lepitino, then shifted back to Browne. "Are you really going back? I thought Mulligan was your friend—Zable even thinks that you . . ."

"That I was in on it? Wrong. P.S., Mulligan hasn't got any, and doesn't want any friends. Not anymore. I'm doing what you should do, get out before you get dealt Big Casino." Browne started toward the door. "Now, gentlemen, good night and good luck, I've got a date with a big bird in the morning."

Rice stood at the open door for a moment. "Thanks for the advice, Lieutenant. Here's some for you. If Zable finds out you've been meeting with Mulligan, or know where he is, he'll be putting the squeeze on you."

"I saw Mr. Zable earlier tonight. He was hip-deep in cops. One of those cops is a pal of mine. Tomorrow I'm going to kiss that cop goodbye, then adios Salt Lake City. I think Mr. Zable will have other things on his mind, but thanks anyhow. And now as they say in France, *bonsoir,* Johnny."

The sun topped out bright but gentle above the east canyon wall and spread its light and warmth softly across the trees and grass and wild flowers below.

Mulligan was awake at first light. It would be a long day and possibly his last, but he had faced that prospect before, too often. And as he had said last night, he would face what lay ahead alone. Claire was out of his life. Annie was dead. He had cut the ties with Keyes and the company. He had sent Browne away, and he would make sure that Abbey Bain was gone before he lit the fuse of his plan.

Clad only in his faded khaki pants, he carried a steaming cup of coffee to Abbey who lay asleep. He sat on the bed gently and held the cup near her face allowing the fragrance to drift. She stirred. She smiled.

"There's only one thing," she murmured with her eyes still closed, "that I like better than coffee."

"Donuts?"

She opened her eyes. Slowly she sat up and took the cup. She wore nothing.

"Mulligan, no matter what happens, I'll always think of one thing about you. You make the best cup of coffee in town." Abbey took a sip, savored the brew in her mouth for a moment, then swallowed. "Make that the world. Have you had breakfast?"

"Yep."

"Let me guess. Coffee, piece of toast with marmalade."

"I don't like that."

"What?"

"Our alliance is falling into a pattern of predictability. Next thing you know, you'll get bored."

"Let's see." She put the coffee cup on the sawed-off log that served as a bed stand, placed both arms around his shoulders, and pressed her mouth against his. The kiss was long and tender and laced with memories of their nights together.

"Not bored yet," she said finally. "How about you?"

"Not even a little bit."

"As the song says 'we've only just begun.' " Her fingers moved from his shoulders to his chest and softly across, then downward. "I never did find out about these scars."

"And I never found out about this." He lifted the sheet aside and touched her thigh.

"I'll tell you all about it. It's a tattoo."

"No kidding."

"And it hasn't been there very long."

"How long?" His thumb moved along the imprint.

"Since I found out about . . . since I found out. Do that some more."

"Okay. Why a butterfly?"

"It's the story of my life. When I was a kid, I wasn't very pretty—like a caterpillar inside its shell. And after a time the shell split open, and before long I was looking into a mirror and there was something happening, something nice. At first the wings were damp and crumpled, but then they dried and spread and I was able to fly away from the shell like a butterfly. That's when I learned that butterflies don't live very long. What do you know about butterflies, Mulligan?"

"Not much. Go ahead and tell me."

"They use camouflage to hide from their enemies."

"So do soldiers."

"And they're poisonous if you eat them."

"For every poison there's an antidote. What else?"

"If they're lucky, they live long enough to find a mate."

"Ah, ha, that's me. The lucky mate."

"No don't say that."

"Why not?"

"Because a male butterfly will die shortly after mating."

"Always?"

"As far as I know."

"Know what?"

"What?"

"You don't know nothing about butterflies." He started to pull away. "I'll be back in a while."

"Where are you going?" She put her arms around him again, pressed him against her breasts and kissed him.

"To plant some seeds," he said.

She still held him close and kissed him again. "Is there any solid reason why I can't go with you?"

This time he drew her against his body, held her for a moment, and moved with her against the flat of the bed. "I guess not."

Her body was warm and wanting. Her hand slipped beneath the wrinkled faded khakis. "Speaking of planting seeds . . ."

Chapter 30

Comprising one of the largest, deepest, man-made pits in the world, CopperScott was played out and had been closed for nearly a year.

There was a sign attached to the gate of the chain-link fence.

> COPPERSCOTT MINE
> DANGER
> NO TRESPASSING

The vast multicolored excavation was ridged with circular ribbons of roads, on which stood tracks, shafts, huge round tanks atop wooden pilings, corrugated sheds, drills, and other equipment that had conceded its usefulness.

Copper, the ancient metal, had been mined for thousands of years before Christ, first in Cyprus from which came the metal's name, then extensively in Europe and

Africa, in Russia and South America. In North America the first mines were dug in Michigan's Lake Superior region and westward through Montana, Nevada, and Utah.

CopperScott was owned and operated by Hamish Scott and then his heirs for nearly a hundred years. But even with the advent of more modern mining techniques and equipment, the price of labor, refining, and shipping had implemented the economic law of diminishing returns, and it no longer paid to dig the dappled ores of chalcopyrite, chalcocite, malachite, and azurite that were yielded into copper.

So CopperScott took its place among the ghosts of the West. Some equipment and vehicles still stood about in disrepair. Peeling and rusted, they were not worth moving. Even the junkmen had turned their backs on what remained.

Just over an hour ago, Mulligan had taken a hacksaw from the tool kit and cut through the lock that served as little more than a token guardian of the remnants below. The chief concern of the authorities was that children would trespass themselves into trouble. But it seemed that children had better places to play. Mulligan was the first trespasser in months, and he brought Abbey Bain with him.

Abbey had followed and silently watched as he removed the contents of the K-kit one by one and concealed them in various areas until his work was done.

Mulligan had also taken the time to remove a set of pitted license plates from one of the abandoned vehicles.

And then the moving speck of jeep crept like an ant

from the floor of the pit along one of the craggy roads winding upward.

It was midmorning when Mulligan and Abbey returned to the cabin. Mulligan was his laconic self, his mind a battlefield playing out the desperate plan.

He had hauled his arsenal from the cabin and set the guns, rifles, and ammunition on the back floorboard of the jeep and covered them with a blanket—all except for the Beretta in his belt.

Abbey sipped from a mug of coffee and watched as he removed the tarp from the Prelude. "Get in," he said, "and make sure it'll start."

She did. It did.

Mulligan then removed the Prelude's license plates and screwed on the pitted plates from CopperScott. "These'll get you to the airport." He handed her a packet of genuine hundreds. "Here's some money—"

"I don't need any money."

"Here's some money," he repeated. "If I'm not at the Fairmont by Friday—"

"Mulligan, be there."

"*Dolan*. If I'm not, you'll read about it. Get the Salt Lake City papers every day."

"Mulligan . . ." Abbey kissed him. He broke away.

"I've got to call Zable and beat them back."

"Mulligan . . ."

"Apaches and Mulligan never say goodbye." He turned, picked up the briefcase filled with counterfeit, and climbed into the jeep.

* * *

Zable's fist snapped against Rice's jaw just below his ear and knocked him into an overstuffed chair. Also present were Lepitino, Pryor, and Raskin.

"Tell me about your buddy Browne."

Rice tried to shake the buzzing out of his brain. "There's nothing to tell, for Christ's sake. I was just pumping him about Mulligan."

"Making a deal!"

"No."

"No, huh? You pumped him yesterday at the bar and this morning at his hotel room. What did you find out? He's in it with Mulligan . . ."

"No."

"Everything's 'no' with you, well how about this for a 'yes.' He knows where Mulligan is."

"He and Mulligan had a beef. Even if he did know, Mulligan's not the kind to roost in one place very long. Besides, Browne's going back to Vegas this morning."

"He's still at his hotel. Bevo just called."

"I tell you he's leaving . . ."

The phone rang.

Rice and Lepitino looked at each other as Zable walked over and lifted the receiver.

"Yeah?"

"Zable?"

"Yeah."

"This is Mulligan. Did you get the hundred dollar bill I left you?"

"Asshole."

"If you want the rest of them come to the CopperScott Mine in two hours. Come alone."

Mulligan hung up. So did Zable. He looked at Rice and the others.

"Get all the boys. This asshole just signed his death warrant."

Mulligan had called from a public phone not far from the mine. That left him plenty of time to drive to CopperScott and get ready.

Chapter 31

Mulligan fired up a Montecruz as he drove the jeep toward the mine.

Rarely did he inhale the smoke from his cigar. But now he did. Deeply. He let it filter into his lungs and through his system. It made him feel good and alive, as he had felt when he heard the sound of Zable's voice on the telephone.

Mulligan could recognize the look of fear when he saw it. He could not see Zable's face when they spoke. But fear also has a smell ... and a sound. There was something in the sound of Zable's raspy voice that betrayed the bravado in the epithet he had uttered.

Mulligan knew that Zable was a killer. He had killed Annie and who knew how many others.

But the kind of killing that Zable did, did not necessarily require courage. Zable did not kill as a soldier kills—or even as a hunter kills.

A soldier often faces the enemy, charges a hill or an emplacement—attacks a position that has defensive firepower. In each case, there is the challenge of retaliation from an armed and ready enemy. Deadly retaliation.

And a hunter's prey can strike back with tooth and claw and horn. The wounded animal, though torn and bleeding, will counter and, with the soaring strength of desperation, try to kill the hunter.

The kind of killing that a soldier or a hunter does requires some element of bravery.

But Zable's kind of killing was different. Zable's victims were too often the unsuspecting, the unwary, the unprepared. And, as in Annie's case, the innocent.

It did not tax a killer's courage to take human life the way Zable took it. To shoot from cover. To confront an unarmed man, or, as with Annie, a defenseless woman.

In that last instant Annie had had to know that Zable was going to kill her. Mulligan now quivered at the thought of that moment. But he knew his sister. He knew that in her last hopeless effort she'd spit in Zable's face.

But Mulligan had other plans for Zable's face. If he could get close enough. He could pop Zable's eyes out of their sockets. With the butt of his palm Mulligan could drive the bone of Zable's nose into his brain.

In the doing Mulligan was prepared to make an even trade. His life for Zable's. Mulligan had never seen a dead man with a smile on his face. But if he killed Zable, and himself died in the doing, he'd die smiling.

As he steered the jeep onto the road to the mine, Mulligan looked at his hands and hoped they would get the chance to do their work on Zable.

But he did not underestimate the odds—or Zable's ability. Yes, there had been the trace of fear in Zable's voice. But only a fool is fearless.

Courage is being afraid to do something—then doing it.

Mulligan heard the faint sound of a church bell. Of course. It was Sunday. Church bells were sounding all over Salt Lake City. All over the country. All over the world.

But dogs don't know it's Sunday. And often neither do soldiers. Calendars don't count. The machinery of war works seven days a week, day and night. There is no time-out for war. No time-out for killing. Soldiers don't rest on the seventh day, and neither do killers. Church bells do not signify sanctuary in the game of death.

Wherever Zable was at this moment, he, too, could hear the church bells peal.

The poet was right.

"... *Never send to know for whom the bell tolls. It tolls for thee.*"

That's right Zable, it tolls for thee, you son of a bitch, Mulligan thought. And maybe it tolls for me.

Sunday's a good day to die. To live no more forever.

"Everybody dies." Johnny Garfield said it in *Body and Soul.* Nobody lives forever. Everybody dies forever. Mulligan was ready to die. Not willing—but ready.

He had done and experienced more than his share of almost everything. Of sorrow and pain.

Sorrow. For his mother and father's death and the scores of listed and nameless deaths he had been responsible for—including the death of his sister.

And pain. His scarred body was a living testament to the pain of his profession. Professions.

Athlete. Soldier. Spook.

Another line from *Body and Soul* came to Mulligan's mind. When Lilli Palmer touched Garfield's face, scarred and stitched from all his fights in the ring, Garfield smiled and said, "In every fight you get something."

From the many encounters Mulligan had faced, too often he, too, had something left on his body—wounds that had healed into scars.

And he, too, had inflicted wounds. Often fatal.

He had had more than his share of victories. From the football fields to the fields of open warfare. And on the covert missions Keyes had assigned—from Washington to the ends of the earth.

More than his share of defeats. From Vietnam to Laos to Salt Lake City.

And more than his share of females. From the first, Cathy at Woodward High School, to Frances Fetzer, the beautiful enigma, to Abbey Bain, the beautiful butterfly.

Yes. Mulligan was ready.

All the encounters in all the years of his life had led him to this day.

The medals, the money, the guilt, the glory—yes, "the paths of glory lead but to the grave"—but so do the paths of shame and cowardice and compromise. There would be no compromise today. Not with Zable and not with whomever Zable would bring with him.

That other set of reflexes had taken over again. Reflexes honed for revenge and retribution. For destruction and death.

He felt that surge of readiness and confidence. His body was prepared. His mind clearer than it had ever been.

And that was when he knew that he had dropped his guard.

Mulligan tossed the butt of the Montecruz out of the jeep.

Chapter 32

Mulligan had parked the jeep at the side of a corrugated tin shed in the bowels of the pit. The structure was approachable from the front and two sides. The rear was sheltered by a huge mound.

Inside, Mulligan had laid out his arsenal on the long wooden table in the middle of the room. The centerpiece of the rifles was a Smith and Wesson M-76 submachine gun from the days and nights in Vietnam. Based on the Swedish SMG, the 76 had a folded stock, a 700–750 cyclic rate, an 8-inch barrel, and a magazine of 36 rounds of 9-mm. Range to hit man-size targets, 100–125 meters. Only 6,000 units were manufactured. This was one of them. A half-dozen magazines were lined up near the weapon.

There were two other rifles on the table, both Winchesters; a 94XTR with a 24-inch barrel and a 7-shot magazine, and a 94 side-eject carbine with a 6-shot tubular magazine. Both fired .30-.30s. Mulligan had a plentiful supply.

Two .357 Magnums were included in the collection, plus

Ted Sahadi's 9-mm Beretta that Mulligan had tucked in his belt.

Also on the table were the briefcase and the five inches by seven inches leather kit, now open. The capsules were gone and the aerial fully extended.

As Mulligan picked up the 76 and thumbed the selector switch from safe to semi-auto, he reacted to a sound, moved toward the window, and looked out.

He saw a car spewing a funnel of copper-colored dust, racing down a road toward the shed. The car was Abbey Bain's Prelude.

"I called your house and your wife said you were down here. Made a bet with myself on whether you were cheating on her or bucking for a promotion. I see I was wrong again."

"Don't just stand there, Reverend Browne. Come in and finish your sermon."

"I'm finished, Ole. On my way back to Vegas. Plane doesn't leave for a couple of hours so I thought I'd stop by."

"Want some coffee? Fresh from yesterday."

"No thanks. And thanks for calling me last night and ... everything else."

"Hell, yes. Maybe I can come to your town and bring you some of my troubles sometime."

"Anytime. Ole, about Mulligan ..."

"What about him?"

"Nothing, I guess ... Well, *hej då* They shook hands and Browne started to move toward the door.

"By the way, Lieutenant," Olsen picked up a sheet from

his desk, "that make you asked for just came off the computer."

Browne stopped, moved back, and took the sheet. "Abbey Bain?"

"Right."

Browne studied the sheet, not for long. "Chicago! Holy shit," he said, "she's one of them!"

She parked the Prelude near the jeep and raced toward the entrance of the shed. Mulligan, still holding the 76, opened the door and Abbey rushed in. He closed the door and looked at her.

"Don't say it, Mulligan; let me talk! You can't do this alone. We probably can't do it together. But together the odds are a lot shorter. Now I can shoot better than I can drive. Give me a gun."

"Why?" Mulligan spoke quietly. "So you can shoot me in the back? That still won't get you the money. And that's what you've been after."

He thumbed the selector from semi-auto back to safe and set the 76 on the table. For a time there was no sound within the shed. No movement. Then Abbey took a step toward him.

"How much do you know?"

"I know you never knew Annie. But you were good. Very good. I knew there was something wrong, but I didn't want to believe it. Maybe that's why it didn't hit me till I was on my way down here."

"What?"

"Coffee. You and Annie drinking coffee together. She hated coffee. Couldn't stand the smell of a cup."

"Want to hear the rest of it?"

"The rest doesn't matter."

"It does to me. You see, Mulligan, I was a whore. Phil Keelo's high-priced whore. There are more polite words for it, but why bother? I knew that someday the price would drop. Keelo's the big man in Chicago, and he gets a regular delivery from Vegas—except that this time Harry Kemp was going to snatch the five million before it got there. It was my idea."

"And the two of you would disappear into the sunset."

"But there was a snag. The car broke down, and then you came along . . ."

"That call Harry made from Flo's, you were on the other end. That's how you knew about me."

"That's right." She nodded. "And I picked up more listening to Keelo talk to Vegas."

"So with Harry dead and me with the money, you decided to switch partners. You found out about Annie and made up that cockamamie story about dying and all that bullshit about butterflies—what's the real story on the butterfly? Did Keelo get his gun off—"

"Maybe you're right, Mulligan." She sighed. "Maybe the rest doesn't matter."

"It probably doesn't." He pointed outside. "Because here they come."

Mulligan picked up the 76 and moved toward a window. Abbey followed.

Chapter 33

Three vehicles approached: the Lincoln; an oversize, high-wheel pickup; and a Dodge Caravan. The Lincoln was in the lead, doing about thirty. It slowed down two hundred yards from the shed. So did the others.

Inside, Mulligan watched as the vehicles fanned out, then stopped. Once more he thumbed the safety on the 76.

"Go on, beat it," he said to Abbey. "They're not after you. You can still square yourself with 'em, no matter what it takes."

"Nothing I want out there."

"There's no future in here."

"I don't care. Mulligan, it started out the way you said, but—"

"Mulligan!" Zable's harsh voice echoed from outside. "Mulligan, you hear me?"

Mulligan stepped to the window and smashed what was left of the broken pane with the stock of the 76.

Zable stood on the far side of the Lincoln. The rest of

the men, all armed, were also outside, except for the drivers still behind the steering wheels.

"Zable!" Mulligan's voice came from the shed. "You're early!"

"Didn't want to keep you waiting here all alone. You are alone, aren't you Mulligan?"

"I see that you're not."

"I brought a few friends with a few guns. Now, Mulligan, let's cut out the shit. Just toss out the money and we take off. You keep a hundred grand for your trouble."

"What about my sister?"

"What about Crago?" Zable croaked back. "We're even-Steven. Toss out the money."

"You want money?" Mulligan walked to the briefcase and flipped it open. He grabbed all the bills his fist could hold, moved back, and flung the hundreds out of the window. *"Here's money!"*

Zable, Rice, and the others watched as the hot wind caught the hundred-dollar bills and swirled them like paper airplanes. The money fluttered about, touched the earth, and some of it was swept away again in all directions.

More bills came flying out of the window.

"Here's some more!" Mulligan taunted.

"He's fucking crazy!" Zable blurted out.

"You want the rest of it, Zable? You and your friends come and get it!" A burst from the 76 scattered the clustered covey of Zable and friends.

"Give it to him!" Zable shouted.

Men and vehicles with drivers still inside dispersed for cover and fired back. Bevo and Cotter—both carried Uzis—blasted away toward the shed. The rest were armed with handguns, ineffective at their present range.

The 9-mm rounds from the Uzis ripped into the tin shed, creating a cascade of sparks and sharp pranging sounds.

Both Mulligan and Abbey ducked away from the two windows, one on each side of the door.

"Mulligan!" Abbey hollered through the bursts, with sententious sarcasm. "May I *please* have a rifle now?"

"Take the carbine." Mulligan let go a pattern of fire from the 76.

"I prefer the XTR."

"Help yourself." Mulligan waved toward the Winchester.

She did.

Mulligan picked up the leather case and tipped the table over, making the guns and ammunition less of a target and scattering the bills from the briefcase onto the floor.

Abbey aimed quickly and fired. Her first shot hit one of the men—Allen—just between the eyes.

"Mother?" Mulligan inquired.

"Mother," Abbey replied and fired again.

Mulligan looked out of the window. In the distance two of the men, Blake and Cotter, had taken refuge behind the wooden pilings that sustained a huge round tank above them. Cotter's Uzi alternated with Bevo's, streaking 9 mms into the shed. Mulligan studied the open leather case and made a selection. He pressed a tiny button next to one of the molds.

"One, two three..." Mulligan counted out loud.

Blake and Cotter could not hear it, but when Mulligan's count reached six, the center ground under the tank erupted in a glorious explosion of fire and smoke. The pilings were converted into flying splinters. What was left of the tank dropped onto what was left of Blake and Cotter and his Uzi.

"Keyes?" Abbey inquired.

"Keyes," Mulligan replied as the debris settled, then he added as he softly tapped the leather case, "the pièce de résistance."

Zable and the others were still staring at the rubble uneasily, wondering how the explosion was detonated, if there would be more? And where?

Zable, Rice, Lepitino, and Bevo with his Uzi were dug in close together. Pryor and Raskin had concealed themselves among the pilings beneath another tank to the right of Zable, but just after the first tank disintegrated, they sought the safety of alternate cover. They ran and ducked behind a mound of scrap.

Escobar and Fanelli had raced forward to the left and crouched behind a stack of oil drums barely within handgun range of the shed. But Abbey's Winchester was well within range. .30-.30s kept both Escobar and Fanelli low to the ground and behind the drums.

Zable motioned for both flanks to move closer while Bevo's Uzi ripped another spray of 9 mms into the badly scarred shed.

As Bevo fired, Pryor and Raskin broke and scrambled to a boulder from which their guns would be more effective. They aimed and shot toward the shed, but before their gunnery could take too much effect, Mulligan pressed another button.

In the interim Escobar and Fanelli scampered toward a bulldozer half buried in the ground. Mulligan pressed a third button.

First the boulder and Pryor and Raskin exploded, and

within seconds the bulldozer detonated into a discomposition of fire, smoke, steel, blood, and shattered bones.

Mulligan set the leather box aside, picked up the 76, and exchanged firepower with Bevo's Uzi in an even contest, until Bevo took a brief time out to insert a new magazine into the Uzi's housing.

Zable and Rice stayed low. Lepitino's face dripped sweat, his hands trembled. Slowly he crept backward. When the 76 ceased its firing, Lepitino turned and sprinted toward the parked van. Before the sprint became a run, Lepitino snapped off the ground, gyrated crazily, and fell with a bullet in his spine.

Zable turned his Magnum toward Rice. "What about you, Johnny? You wanna go someplace?"

Rice cowered. He didn't answer.

Inside, Abbey reloaded the Winchester and looked at Mulligan.

"The ranks are thinning."

"So is the shed."

Another burst from Bevo's Uzi.

"Keep down."

"Mulligan."

"What?"

"Maybe this is as close as we get to Shangri-la."

"Maybe." Mulligan pressed the fourth button.

In six seconds there was another earth-shattering explosion—more flame, smoke, and debris, with some fallout among the survivors but no casualties. There were two dishlike craters within sixty yards of the shed. Mulligan had concealed a capsule within the one on the right. Luckily for Zable, he had ducked into the one on the left.

Mulligan had one remaining capsule, but it was not yet

time to hit the last button. He crouched as Bevo fired again.

Under cover of Bevo's Uzi, Detroit dashed ahead toward a tipped wheelbarrow closer to the shed. He was almost there when a .30-.30 from Abbey's XTR tore away his throat.

"The odds are getting shorter," she said to Mulligan who traded 9 mms with Bevo.

"Mulligan . . ."

"What?"

A smile and a curious look came across Abbey's face. Oblivious of the gunfire, she walked toward Mulligan. "I'm dying for a . . . cup of coffee . . ."

Abbey dropped the Winchester and fell. There was a blood splotch on the left side of her back.

Mulligan knelt and gently turned her face up. He brushed the wisps of blond hair from her eyes. But she never knew it.

Zable wiped the sweat from his face with his left hand. "Bevo!"

"Yeah?"

"Get that sonofabitch outta there."

"How?"

Zable pointed to the oversize pickup. "Ram him. There's not much left of that shed."

"Cover me." Bevo nodded and ran in an uneven zigzag pattern back toward the pickup as Zable and Rice peppered the shed with gunfire.

Mulligan still knelt with Abbey dead in his arms. He heard the roar of an engine and tires grinding over the ground.

He moved to the window and looked out. The pickup

was coming full bore. Bevo, at the wheel, had his foot to the floorboard, his left hand held the Uzi firing on automatic as the truck ripped straight toward the shed.

Mulligan grabbed the leather box, pressed the last button, dropped the box, ran and dove through a side window just as the truck crashed into the door of the shed.

Mulligan hit the ground outside, sprang to his feet, and ran as fast as he could. The shed, the truck, the jeep, and Abbey's car blew into a fiery conflagration of scarred and twisted tin, wood, and steel—and bogus hundred-dollar bills descending like confetti among the ruins.

Rice, gun in hand, walked through the smoke. He saw Mulligan, fired, and missed. Mulligan pulled the Beretta from his belt. Both men fired simultaneously. Rice missed again. Mulligan didn't.

Rice fell face forward onto the blistered ground.

Out of the inferno, Zable, at the wheel of the van, raced the machine toward Mulligan. Mulligan took fast aim, fired, smashed the windshield; and the Caravan skidded to the left, then recovered as Mulligan made for more rugged terrain.

Zable's van ran over Rice's body, front wheels and back, twisting and bouncing the lifeless torso against the hard copper-crusted ground, then continued in its pursuit of Mulligan.

Over the rim of the jagged horizon, out of the sun, dipping into the vast crater, the helicopter arced a hundred yards above the furrowed ground, toward the smoke and dust where the shed had stood.

Detective-Lieutenant Bernard Browne, at the controls of the Bell Jet Ranger, looked below through the black-damp cloud and saw Mulligan running across a set of rusty tracks and toward a craggy uphill section. The van slowed down but humped across the tracks with tires whipstitching into the rims and then coming round again.

Browne accelerated the chopper, dipped, then cut across the front of the van, barely avoiding a collision and forcing the Caravan to veer away.

Mulligan kept running.

The chopper circled and made another close pass at the van, its rotors kicking up dust and umbered dirt that swirled blindingly across the windshield.

Browne swung the bird away from the van toward Mulligan, who slipped the Beretta into his belt, slowed down, and extended both arms skyward as the chopper fluttered toward him.

Zable kept both of his hands on the steering wheel, jammed the accelerator to the floor, and took dead aim at Mulligan.

The streaking van was only yards away when Mulligan grabbed the runner of the chopper and was lifted off the ground as the Caravan's roof barely missed smashing his contracted legs.

Mulligan clung to the runner. Browne slowed the helicopter and motioned for him to climb upward. But Mulligan, still holding on with both hands, motioned with his head and legs for Browne to go after the van.

"Oh, shit," Browne exclaimed to himself, to Mulligan, and to the world.

Nevertheless, while Mulligan dangled, the chopper swerved and dove toward the van.

"Sonofabitch!" Zable swore through rat-thin lips. He looked up and out of the open side window to get a better view of the helicopter's position. The van hit a furrow and Zable almost lost control.

The chopper and Mulligan swooped closer to the dust-caked Caravan ... closer—close enough. Mulligan dropped from the bird to the roof of the van and gripped the luggage rack.

The van shuddered and bounced on the gutted ground with Mulligan shuddering and bouncing on top of it.

He crawled toward the front and reached for his gun. He transferred the Beretta into his left hand and held onto the rack with his right. Mulligan stretched down toward the driver's window and fired inside.

Zable instinctively ducked as the bullet grazed past him and smashed the windshield then ricocheted off off the passenger door. In ducking, Zable twisted the steering wheel. The van crashed into a telephone pole.

The impact threw Mulligan off the top of the van, snapped the pole in half and onto the hood of the Caravan.

Mulligan hit the ground with his left shoulder, still holding the Beretta in his right hand. He rolled to his feet, jammed the gun back in his belt, and ran toward the driver's door which had sprung open. Zable, barely conscious but badly dazed, was slumped at the wheel. Mulligan grabbed Zable and pulled him out.

A hundred feet away, the chopper touched the ground and settled.

Mulligan slammed Zable against the crumpled front fender of the van, near the fallen pole. His right fist smashed into Zable's nose, splintering bone. Blood spewed into the man's open mouth.

"You killed my sister." Mulligan held Zable up to keep him from falling.

The butt of his right palm drove into Zable's forehead. "You killed my sister."

Zable attempted to lift his arms in defense, but it was useless. Mulligan battered Zable's face and body, driven by hate and venom.

This was the last enemy. Zable was all the forces Mulligan had fought against for years. Sometimes face to face. More often unseen and skulking. But Mulligan could see and feel this enemy, this thing that killed without feeling, without emotion. This thing that had brutalized and murdered and desecrated the innocent sister whom Mulligan loved. He would never get at the enemy who hired Zable, just as he could never get at those who hired Rostov, those who planned the slaughters in Vietnam, in Africa, in South America, and all the other places. Those enemies at the top were impervious and immune. This was all the revenge that Mulligan could have.

So with his aching fists he demolished this vile and wicked thing, until Browne twisted him around and Zable dropped.

"Mulligan!" Browne shoved him away.

Mulligan staggered as Browne walked toward him. "Mulligan, it's *over!*" Browne held out his hand.

But Mulligan ripped the gun from his belt and fired in Browne's direction.

The bullet passed between Browne's body and arm— into Zable who had been pointing the Magnum. Browne turned in time to see Walter Zable drop the gun and die. Then the lieutenant looked back at Mulligan.

"Now it's over," said Mulligan.

They walked toward the helicopter in silence until Mulligan said, "Bernard, I thought you left town."

"Missed my plane." Browne smiled.

The chopper lifted off and headed toward the horizon and Salt Lake City.

"Where'd you get this machine?"

"Let's say I confiscated it."

"Well," said Mulligan, "I hate to shoot and run but..."

"Yeah, I know. Send us a post card."

"Us?"

"Louise and me, Mr. and Mrs. Browne."

"I will."

For a few moments there was only the sound of the helicopter engine and rotor.

"You know," Browne said, "she was in on it."

"At the beginning. Later ... I don't know."

"I've got a sheet on her. You want to read it?"

"No." Mulligan shook his head. "I guess I know all I need to know." He looked below at the devastation and the smoldering remnants of the encounter.

"Bernard, how you gonna explain all this?"

"Looks to me like mob warfare." Browne smiled. "Slaughtered each other over some counterfeit money."

Mulligan almost smiled back. In a slow, deliberate motion he playfully arced a punch to Browne's chin. Browne grinned and moved his head with the punch.

The helicopter dipped—and fluttered like a butterfly.

Epilogue

More tanned than he had ever been in his life, Mulligan lay on the oversize beach blanket, his eyes closed under the Porsche Design sunglasses, listening only to the serene sound of the surf and the occasional calls or laughter of the few swimmers in the blue-white waters of the island's cove.

This South Seas' garden had not yet been discovered and developed by civilization's brummagem builders. That would come in the next decade as it came to so many islands and other places. Mulligan, rather Frank Dolan, would be gone by then to some yet unexploited place, or maybe back to the density of civilization where he would be just one more of the many.

There were three clean and comfortable hotels on the island occupied mostly by middle-aged, middle-class vacationers or young and happy honeymooners who had been told of the almost secret island by previous young and happy honeymooners, or by the few travel agents who concerned themselves less with making larger profits by directing their clients to expensive hostelries and more with making their clients content.

But Mulligan did not live at any of the three hotels, although he not infrequently visited two of the bars and frequently dined at one of the hotel restaurants. He had purchased a cottage on three acres just outside the village. The house had two bedrooms, a den, modern kitchen, two baths, and a lanai. It came complete with housekeeper and gardener-handyman. He was halfway through writing a novel, a mystery, but he was in no hurry to finish the second half.

He rose to one elbow, looked out facing the ocean for a few moments, then turned and watched as she walked toward him. He took off his sunglasses.

Even from a distance there was something familiar about her. And if there hadn't been, he still would have watched. Mulligan had seen damned few figures like hers since he'd come to the island, or before.

She wore a green bathing suit and over it a short white terry-cloth robe, open at the front, allowing a bountiful display of the spheres of her body. She strode closer to him on lovely tapered legs. She was tall, with long slender, but strong, hands. Her complexion was Californian. It set off a valentine-shaped face and classic features, except for lips a little too large and too red. She removed her sunglasses. Her eyes were emerald green and lucent, her hair the color of burnished copper.

She stopped only a couple of feet from Mulligan's blanket. From his low angle, Mulligan had an excellent view.

"Hello, stranger." She smiled.

"Hello, yourself. How could you know I was here? On

the other hand," Mulligan reflected, "how could you *not* know? Did Keyes send you?"

"No."

"This is not a coincidence?" The question was rhetorical.

"No."

"Then Keyes has got to have something to do with it."

"Sort of. A week ago Keyes came into the office ninety seconds late. I knew that meant something was wrong."

"Is he okay?"

"One might say that."

"What else might one say?"

"He handed me a piece of paper. 'Miss Fetzer,' he said, 'would you mind typing this up as soon as possible?' "

"And?"

"And I typed it up. It was to the Director. Three sentences, a total of thirty-seven words."

"What did they say?"

"It amounted to 'I quit.' "

"Did he mention why?"

"The usual—'personal reasons.' Twenty minutes later, as he left he said, 'Thank you and goodbye, Miss Fetzer. Please give my best regards to Mulligan.' That's the last time I saw him—and the first time I saw him smile."

"Sorry I missed that."

"Along with his resignation I typed my own ... and here I am."

"Yes, you are." Mulligan looked her up and down. "You want to do anything about it?"

"Yes, I do."

"Is there room enough on that blanket for the two of us?"

"Yes, there is."

She sat close to him. Very close. Her legs touched his. "You don't want me just for my money, do you?"

"What money?" he asked.

"You didn't know that I was worth over thirty million dollars?"

"What?"

"Well, maybe not worth it, but I've got it. Always had. Inherited it from my great-grandfather. He was a robber baron."

"Then why the hell were you working for Keyes?"

"I don't know. Guess it made me feel sort of ... patriotic. Why were you working for him?"

"So I could meet you."

She meshed into his arms and pressed her smooth and tender lips onto his mouth. That same first elevator flush hit Mulligan again. "You know what I think?" he said.

"What?"

"When you reach perfection—level off."

"Now I'll tell you something."

"Tell me."

"I never did get you out of my system." She kissed him again.

"Miss Fetzer" he murmured, and lowered her onto the blanket.

"Call me Frances," she murmured back.

STAY IN-THE-KNOW WITH
PINNACLE'S CONTEMPORARY FICTION

STOLEN MOMENTS (17-095, $4.50)
by Penelope Karageorge
Cosmos Inc. was the place to be. The limitless expense accounts and round-the-world junkets were more than perks. They were a way of life—until Black Thursday. Cosmos' employees, who jockeyed for power, money, and sex, found that life was indeed a game of winners and losers.

DUET (17-130, $4.95)
by Kitty Burns Florey
Even as they took other lovers and lived separate lives, Anna and Will were drawn together time and again, their destinies mingling in a duet of wistful hopes and bittersweet dreams. Unable to move ahead, Anna surrendered at last to the obsession that held her with chains more binding than love, more lasting than desire.

SWITCHBACK (17-136, $3.95)
by Robin Stevenson and Tom Bade
Dorothea was in a movie, starring Vernon Dunbar, the love of her life. She was sure that she had never made that film. Only her granddaughter, Elizabeth, could help prove this fact to her. But Elizabeth could only do this if she could travel back in time.

ENTANGLED (17-059, $4.50)
by Nelle McFather
Three women caught in a tangle of lies and betrayal. And one man held the key to their deepest secrets that could destroy their marriages, their careers, and their lives.

THE LION'S SHARE (17-138, $4.50)
by Julia Kent
Phillip Hudson, the founder of Hawaii's billion-dollar Hudson Corporation, had been a legendary powerhouse in his lifetime. But his power did not end with his sudden death, as his heirs discovered at the reading of his will. Three beautiful women were candidates for Hudson's inheritance, but only one would inherit The Lion's Share.

THE LAST INHERITOR (17-064, $3.95)
by Genevieve Lyons
The magnificent saga of Dan Casey, who rose from the Dublin slums to become the lord and master of the majestic Slievelea. Never seeking love nor asking for it, the strikingly handsome Casey charmed his way into the lives of four unforgettable women who sacrificed everything to make his dreams a reality.

Available wherever paperbacks are sold, or order direct from the Publisher. Send cover price plus 50¢ per copy for mailing and handling to Pinnacle Books, Dept.17-273, 475 Park Avenue South, New York, N.Y. 10016. Residents of New York, New Jersey and Pennsylvania must include sales tax. DO NOT SEND CASH.

ESPIONAGE FICTION BY WARREN MURPHY AND MOLLY COCHRAN

GRANDMASTER (17-101, $4.50)
There are only two true powers in the world. One is goodness. One is evil. And one man knows them both. He knows the uses of pleasure, the secrets of pain. He understands the deadly forces that grip the world in treachery. He moves like a shadow, a promise of danger, from Moscow to Washington — from Havana to Tibet. In a game that may never be over, he is the grandmaster.

THE HAND OF LAZARUS (17-100, $4.50)
A grim spectre of death looms over the tiny County Kerry village of Ardath. The savage plague of urban violence has begun to weave its insidious way into the peaceful fabric of Irish country life. The IRA's most mysterious, elusive, and bloodthirsty murderer has chosen Ardath as his hunting ground, the site that will rock the world and plunge the beleaguered island nation into irreversible chaos: the brutal assassination of the Pope.

Available wherever paperbacks are sold, or order direct from the Publisher. Send cover price plus 50¢ per copy for mailing and handling to Pinnacle Books, Dept.17-273, 475 Park Avenue South, New York, N.Y. 10016. Residents of New York, New Jersey and Pennsylvania must include sales tax. DO NOT SEND CASH.

CRITICALLY ACCLAIMED MYSTERIES FROM ED MCBAIN AND PINNACLE BOOKS!

BEAUTY AND THE BEAST (17-134, $3.95)
When a voluptuous beauty is found dead, her body bound with coat hangers and burned to a crisp, it is up to lawyer Matthew Hope to wade through the morass of lies, corruption and sexual perversion to get to the shocking truth! The world-renowned author of over fifty acclaimed mystery novels is back—with a vengeance.

"A REAL CORKER... A DEFINITE PAGE-TURNER."
—*USA TODAY*

"HIS BEST YET."
—*THE DETROIT NEWS*

"A TIGHTLY STRUCTURED, ABSORBING MYSTERY"
—*THE NEW YORK TIMES*

JACK & THE BEANSTALK (17-083, $3.95)
Jack McKinney is dead, stabbed fourteen times, and thirty-six thousand dollars in cash is missing. West Florida attorney Matthew Hope's questions are unearthing some long-buried pasts, a second dead body, and some gorgeous suspects. Florida's getting hotter by deadly degrees—as Hope bets it all against a scared killer with nothing left to lose!

"ED MCBAIN HAS ANOTHER WINNER."
—*THE SAN DIEGO UNION*

"A CRACKING GOOD READ... SOLID, SUSPENSEFUL, SWIFTLY-PACED"
—*PITTSBURGH POST-GAZETTE*

Available wherever paperbacks are sold, or order direct from the Publisher. Send cover price plus 50¢ per copy for mailing and handling to Pinnacle Books, Dept.17-273, 475 Park Avenue South, New York, N.Y. 10016. Residents of New York, New Jersey and Pennsylvania must include sales tax. DO NOT SEND CASH.

DOCTOR WHO AND THE TALONS OF WENG-CHIANG (17-209, $3.50)
by Terrance Dicks

Doctor Who learns a Chinese magician, the crafty Chang, and his weird midget manikin, Mr. Sin, are mere puppets in the hands of the hideously deformed Greel, posing as the Chinese god, Weng-Chiang. It is Greel who steals the young women; it is Greel who grooms sewer rats to do his bidding—but there is even more, much more.... Will Doctor Who solve the Chinese puzzle in time to escape the terrifying talons of Weng-Chiang?

DOCTOR WHO AND THE MASQUE OF MANDRAGORA (17-224, $3.50)
by Phillip Hinchcliffe

It is the Italian Renaissance during the corrupt reign of the powerful Medicis. Doctor Who, angry because he was forced to land on Earth by the incredible Mandragora Helix, walks right into a Machiavellian plot. The unscrupulous Count Frederico plans to usurp the rightful rule of his naive nephew. This, with the help of Hieronymous, influential court astrologer and secret cult member. Using Hieronymous and his cult members as a bridgehead, the Mandragora Helix intends to conquer Earth and dominate its people! The question is, will Doctor Who prove a true Renaissance man? Will he be able to drain the Mandragora of its power and foil the Count as well?

Available wherever paperbacks are sold, or order direct from the Publisher. Send cover price plus 50¢ per copy for mailing and handling to Pinnacle Books, Dept.17-273, 475 Park Avenue South, New York, N.Y. 10016. Residents of New York, New Jersey and Pennsylvania must include sales tax. DO NOT SEND CASH.